Walking
with
Harry
in
Chamonix

Walking
with
Harry
in
Chamonix

John Winter

Copyright © 2013 John W. Winter

The moral right of the author has been asserted.

Apart from any fair dealing for the purposes of research or private study, or criticism or review, as permitted under the Copyright, Designs and Patents Act 1988, this publication may only be reproduced, stored or transmitted, in any form or by any means, with the prior permission in writing of the publishers, or in the case of reprographic reproduction in accordance with the terms of licences issued by the Copyright Licensing Agency. Enquiries concerning reproduction outside those terms should be sent to the publishers.

Matador
Unit 9, Priory Business Park
Kibworth Beauchamp
Leicester LE8 0RX, UK
Tel: (+44) 116 279 2299
Fax: (+44) 116 279 2277
Email: books@troubador.co.uk
Web: www.troubador.co.uk/matador

ISBN 978 178306 0061

British Library Cataloguing in Publication Data.
A catalogue record for this book is available from the British Library.

Typeset in 11pt StempelGaramond Roman by Troubador Publishing Ltd, Leicester, UK

Matador is an imprint of Troubador Publishing Ltd

Printed and bound in the UK by TJ International, Padstow, Cornwall

Un grand merci
 to Jean-Pierre and Marie-Françoise Bichat who first introduced me to the delights of walking in Chamonix.

 to Didier, Théo and Geneviève Matteudi – who always gave a warm welcome to Anglo-French Walks groups at Les Cîmes in Les Praz.

 And not least to my wife, Freda, for her help and encouragement.

CONTENTS

	Preface	ix
1.	Harry's dilemma	1
2.	O.L.'s euphoria	11
3.	Harry re-invents himself	20
4.	O.L.'s amazement	29
5.	Countdown	44
6.	Sod's law	52
7.	First impresions	63
8.	*Le Chalet du Chapeau*	74
9.	*La Mer de Glace*	98
10.	*Le Lac Blanc*	117
11.	*L'Aiguille du Midi*	139
12.	*Le Glacier du Tour*	158
13.	*La Jonction*	188

PREFACE

Thurston Ramblers, like most rambling clubs, is a mixture of strong walkers and plodders with the majority somewhere in between. The strong walkers need no arm-twisting when the club is invited to Chamonix by Monique, Mavis's pen-friend. The plodders are intimidated by the very mention of walking in the Alps while the majority express interest but want to know more.

Among the strong walkers is the club's zealous president, Mrs Olive Lavinia Jonstone, referred to as O.L. by Harry Birch, plodder-in-chief and a constant thorn in her flesh. Whether the fragile truce between them can survive is a constant souce of speculation amomg the rank and file.

Sweating up mountains is not Harry's scene. Neither O.L. nor anyone else in the club expects him to sign up for Chamonix. Yet he does! 'Walking with Harry in Chamonix' – a sequel to 'Walking with Harry' – is the story of how he re-invents himself, how the club prepares for walking in the Alps and how its outspoken members, plodders and striders alike, always ready for a laugh, fare when they get there, guided by Monique, herself a Chamoniarde and a fund of local knowledge.

HARRY'S DILEMMA

How long would the truce last? Had Harry and O.L. finally buried the hatchet? Among the rank and file of Thurston Ramblers, opinions differed. The optimists, led by Gladys who had a foot in both camps, thought the omens were good. Had they not been chatting like long-lost buddies in Wasdale Inn after the ill-fated walk to Scafell? The realists, led by Harry's pal Bert, took the view that this display of mutual respect could not possibly last and that hostilities would soon be resumed: laid-back Harry and up-tight O.L. were never going to see eye to eye on the subject of walking – or of much else. Which of these opinions was nearer the mark was to be revealed at the club's AGM in November at the Rose and Crown.

'And how is Mr Birch this cold and frosty evening? Fit and well, I hope.' came a shrill voice as Harry entered the room, Guinness in hand. The voice was unmistakenly that of the club's president, Mrs Olive Lavinia Jonstone.

Harry almost dropped his glass. Never before had O.L. shown the slightest concern about his state of health. He mustered a weak smile, said he was fine and hoped the feeling was mutual. Well pleased by this exchange of pleasantries, Gladys nudged Mavis: it looked as if the truce was holding. Bert, unconvinced, raised an eyebrow but said nothing.

The AGM began smoothly enough. O.L. wisely made no reference to her last year's proposal of an admissions policy, ridiculed by Harry. Nor, in her review of the year's activities, did she mention Harry's 'Mystery Walk' which had appalled her, the trick he had played on her in Snowdonia or his wine-drinking in Teesdale which she had so vigorously objected to. What had impressed her was the club's *esprit de corps*, particularly on Joe's walk on Pillar and her own walk to see the sunrise on Scafell. They had every right to feel pleased with the way they had coped wth bad weather and the accident to Joyce.

Harry was puzzled. O.L. seemed to have mellowed. There was nothing in her speech he found objectionable. No crazy proposals, no allusions to amblers and geriatrics in the club, no talk of following in Mr Wainwright's footsteps. Harry smelled a rat. The change was too abrupt. There was a glint in her eye that made him wary: the same manic glint he'd observed when she had enthused about sleeping under boulders below Scafell. It was not until she came to Any Other Business that the reason for her high spirits became clear.

'Ladies and gentlemen,' she began, 'I received this week a very interesting letter. You will remember, no doubt, when Monique, Mavis's pen friend, joined us on our walk in Teesdale earlier in the year.'

'Remember Monique?' interrupted Bert. 'Harry can't stop talking about her, can you Harry? That photo you took at Low Force, the one with Monique perched on a rock by the Tees, you've had it blown up, haven't you? On your bedroom wall, isn't it? First thing you see when you wake up every morning!'

'Oh, you mean that one, Bert,' replied Harry casually. 'The one that won a first in the camera club exhibition. I seem to recall you asked me for a copy.'

O.L. took a dim view of being interrupted by facetious and irrelevant remarks when she had a serious announcement to make.

'If I may continue,' she went on coldly, losing some of her earlier sunniness. 'I have just received a letter from Monique in which she thanks us all, very profusely, for our warm hospitality and the lovely walk in Teesdale. She then goes on to say, and this is the part that I found especially interesting, that she would be delighted to welcome Thurston Ramblers to her home town of Chamonix in the French Alps during next year's summer holidays.' O.L. paused to allow for the smiles, nods and comments to subside before going on.

'Furthermore, Monique is offering to arrange our accommodation and lead our walks. She says there are a great number of spectacular walks to choose from in the Chamonix Valley.' Putting Monique's letter on the table, she continued, 'As you may or may not know, the Chamonix Valley is overlooked on both sides by high mountains and glaciers. The jewel in the crown is, of course, the snow-capped Mont-Blanc, the roof of Europe at 4,810 metres. That's almost five times the height of Scafell Pike! Just imagine!'

O.L. couldn't suppress her excitement. Her proudest achievement so far had been climbing Snowdon, a mere 1085 metres. In Chamonix itself, she would be at 1036 metres. The challenges that lay ahead were exhilarating. She had already envisaged herself, together with Mike and

Joe, the club's hard men, on the snowy summit of Mont-Blanc.

'I really think Monique's kind offer is too good to turn down,' she went on. 'I'm sure you will agree with me that it's the chance of a lifetime.' O.L. didn't wait to see if they agreed with her or not, assuming automatically that any serious rambler worth his salt would jump at the chance of walking in the Alps. 'Now, to get things moving, I propose that we opt for the last week of August. I will draw up a schedule of training walks in the Dales and Lakes in the weeks preceding. Any problems?'

In the stunned silence that followed, Harry was the first to find his voice.

'Yes, Olive, I've a problem, several problems in fact.'

'Not worried about altitude sickness, are you, Harry?' cried Bert.

This veiled allusion to Harry's preference for low level walks was not lost on O.L. who burst into a spasm of laughter. Harry forced a smile but it was clear to Gladys that tension between the two was re-surfacing; the truce was beginning to look fragile.

'Before you have us booking flights,' he went on briskly, 'a few facts about the walks wouldn't come amiss. Do you propose to give Monique a free hand in choosing them or do we have any say in the matter? Climbing 500 metres or more every day for a week, isn't my idea of a holiday.and I'm sure I'm not the only one.'

Sensing that Harry was back in bolshie mode, O.L. reacted sharply.

'I never thought for a moment that walking in the Alps would appeal to you, Mr Birch. That would be well outside your comfort zone as we all know. As for choosing the walks, I'm sure we'll be able to come to an agreement with Monique.'

'I think I can help there,' interposed Mavis. 'When I visited Monique last year, she showed me a guide book and map about walks in the Chamonix Valley. It's called *Sentiers du Mont-Blanc* and the walks are all graded. If you like, I'll ask Monique to send me a copy.'

O.L. beamed and thanked Mavis. A guide book was just what they needed. The committee could draw up a short-list and then ask Monique what she thought of their choices.

'You do realise, Olive, that the book is in French. If that's a problem, I think I'd be able to give you a rough translation. Or maybe I wouldn't be needed now that Harry's going to evening classes in French. I remember he made quite an impression on Monique in Teesdale, *n'est-ce pas*, Harry? You could be a big hit in Chamonix.'

'Afraid that's unlikely, Mavis.' came the reply. 'I doubt if I'll be gracing you with my presence. As we all know, to quote our president, I would be well out of my comfort zone.'

O.L. could hardly conceal her relief. Harry Birch in Chamonix would be a liability. He would undermine her authority and his negative attitude could rub off on the group. They'd be better off without him. Mavis, on the other hand, seemed genuinely regretful.

'Pity about that, Harry. Maybe you'll change your mind if I show you the Official Guide to Chamonix. Actually, you could download it yourself from the net or ask the Tourist Office to post it to you. It's a mine of information and some of the photos in it are awesome.'

At the mention of photos, Harry pricked up his ears. Photography interested him much more than sweating up mountains. Yes, he would like to see the Guide, he told Mavis, but he didn't think it would change his mind. Gladys also expressed doubts: at the age of 70+. she couldn't see herself striding up mountains and crossing glaciers. Nor could Joyce, less than half the age of Gladys but considerably more rotund. Betty had already heard inspiring reports about Chamonix from her colleague Mavis, and was eager to learn more. Penny too was interested: she had only recently come across a beautifully illustrated book about the Tour of Mont-Blanc in the library where she worked and the possibility of seeing a golden eagle, choughs and snow buntings was an added attraction.

O.L. had never doubted that retired policeman Mike and his equally fit friend Joe would be up for it. Both had done some climbing in the Chamonix Valley twenty years ago and spoke highly of the magnificent mountain scenery. Ex-army sergeant Bill and his fellow Welshman Syd had climbed in Snowdonia and both nodded approval. In the absence of Harry, Bert offered to keep an eye on Monique whereupon Bill offered to keep an eye on Bert.

O.L. was well satisfied with the way things had turned out. She now had the nucleus of a group, a mixture of crag-hoppers and plodders but without stragglers like her accident-prone friend Gladys and her *bête noire* Harry Birch.

'I propose, ladies and gentlemen, that we resume our discussion at the next meeting in two weeks' time. By then, Mavis will have received the guide book and map from Monique and we'll be able to decide on possible walks. Suppose you also asked her, Mavis, to send a few copies of the Chamonix Official Guide for those of us who don't have access to the internet. Perhaps you would bring the book you mentioned, Penny. In the meantime, I will write to Monique to accept her kind offer and suggest the last week of August for our visit. I trust that meets with your approval.'

In his self-appointed role as Leader of the Opposition, Harry felt obliged to query her choice of dates.

'You don't beat about the bush, Olive, I'll say that for you,' he began. 'What makes you assume we'd be free the last week in August? We're not all retired, you know. Some of us have fixed holidays and some have to keep to a holiday rota. Some of us may have already booked a holiday for that week and others might have family commitments like grand-children to look after, weddings to attend, anniversaries ... '

O.L. cut him short.

'Really, Mr Birch, I'm perfectly well aware some people may have conflicting engagements but if we ask everyone which week they prefer, we'll never get anywhere. We're looking nine months ahead, time enough for most, if not all of us, to arrange to be free for that week. Now if there's nothing else, I will declare the meeting closed.'

Not to be so easily silenced, Harry said there was something else.

'I'd like to know what sort of accommodation

Monique's proposing. Not, I trust, one of those refuges – mountain huts, bothies, call them what you will – that I've read about. You know the sort of thing: bunk beds in unisex dormitories for about twenty people snoring their heads off. All the windows closed, the smell of sweaty bodies, nowhere to undress or put your gear, washing and shaving in cold water, toilets without seats. I could go on.'

'Please don't, Harry.' cried Mavis, 'You've said enough. Anyway, they're not all as primitive as you make out. I stayed in one last year that was almost like a hotel. I'm sure Monique wouldn't suggest a refuge for us.'

'I just hope you're right, Mavis,' replied Harry. 'A decent hotel with hot showers, comfortable beds and good food would be a minimum requirement for me – if I were going, that is. Which brings me to the question of cost. A week's half-board in a decent hotel plus travel expenses, whether by train or air, is going to cost an arm and a leg. Frankly, I'd sooner spend a week nearer home, on Anglesey for example. They tell me there are some lovely coastal paths round Anglesey and the sea air's very bracing.'

O.L. tried hard to keep her cool but found it difficult. She might have known he would try to rock the boat. Speaking slowly and deliberately in an icy tone, she counter-attacked.

'Why you should be so interested in these matters, Mr Birch, I have no idea. You've already said we shan't have the pleasure of your company in Chamonix. If you personally want to stroll along the beaches of Anglesey, so be it. There are those among us, the majority I might say, who prefer something more challenging. As for your premature concerns about accommodation, you might have waited to hear what Monique has to suggest. It certainly won't be like the refuge you so luridly described. Your remarks about cost were equally alarming – and unfounded. There are cheap flights to Geneva, the nearest airport to Chamonix, and hotels in France are less expensive if anything than they are here. I now declare the meeting closed.'

Outside the pub, Gladys expressed her dismay to Mavis. Harry had obviously been winding Olive up and she had sharply rebuffed him. Bert was right when he said the truce between them would be short-lived. Mavis shrugged her shoulders: Harry and Olive had had spats like this before and, in her opinion, secretely enjoyed them: they shouldn't be taken too seriously.

Mavis said good night to Gladys and rushed off to catch Harry who was just getting into his car: she had something important to tell him.

'Listen, Harry, you've got to have a re-think about Chamonix. We'd all miss you – except Olive of course. And who's going to rein her in if you're not there? When Monique sends me that guide book, I want to give you a preview before I pass it on to Olive. I want you to see how many walks are graded *'sans difficulté.'* There are dozens of them, well within your scope. On both sides of the valley, there are balcony paths involving no more than 250 metres of climbing. Other walks start from high up but the great thing about Chamonix is the number of cable cars, gondolas and ski-lifts which take you right into the mountains. Think of all the stunning photos you could take without even breaking sweat.'

Monique paused. She could see that Harry was interested. To whet his appetite further, she told him about the rack and pinion railway up to the *Mer de Glace*, the ice grotto in the glacier and the awe-inspiring mountains in close proximity. It was a photographer's dreamland. Harry was now all ears. This was the time for Mavis to play her trump card.

'By the way,' she added casually, 'I had an e-mail yesterday from Monique. She told me she'd written to Olive inviting us to Chamonix. You got a mention. She said that she was very much looking forward to seeing you again.'

Harry was not often short of words. After a lengthy pause, he muttered,

'Really, that's interesting. I suppose it would be a pity to disappoint her. Give me a ring when you get that book. Maybe I will have a re-think after all.'

On her way home, Mavis was sure of one thing: Thurston Ramblers would not be going to Chamonix without Harry Birch.

O.L.'S EUPHORIA

At the next meeting two weeks later, O.L. was cock-a-hoop. After Mavis had distributed copies of the Chamonix Guide sent to her by the tourist office, she announced briskly:

'Ladies and gentlemen, I have more good news for you. Monique has told me on the telephone that her uncle owns a hotel near Chamonix. He has generously offered us a special half-board rate of 350 euros for the week!'

O.L.'s euphoria was not shared by Bert, never keen to open his wallet.

'Doesn't sound like a big deal to me, Olive. That's about £300! A small fortune!'

'Nothing you can't afford, Bert.' chipped in Harry, 'You'll make that in a couple of days putting washers on taps. I wish I'd taken up plumbing when I was a lad.'

O.L. tried to stem the chit-chat by repeating that this was a very generous offer. It was a two star hotel and they were being given a 30% reduction. What was more, the hotel had a very good reputation locally for its cuisine.

Although more of a gourmand than a gourmet, Bert was impressed by this news. While he was enjoying the delights of French cooking, he would spare a thought for Harry slumming it over pie and peas in the corner café back home.

Harry retaliated by pointing out that, as far as he

knew, hotel rooms in France didn't provide brewing-up facilities. How would Bert survive a week without his early morning cuppa? Worse still, he could forget about his customary breakfast fry-ups! Bye-bye bacon, egg, sausage, mushrooms and beans; hello *croissant* and *baguette*.

O.L.'s patience was beginning to wear thin. They were like overgrown school boys, those two. Thank goodness she wouldn't have to put up with their infantile sense of humour in Chamonix. On his own, Bert would be tolerable.

What O.L. didn't know at this point was that Harry had changed his mind. Mavis had known this intuitively two weeks ago but had left it to him to break the news. Harry bided his time as O.L, ignoring the interruptions, called for order and went on.

'Of course, we'll have to tell the hotel how many rooms we need so I'd like to know who is sharing with whom and how many prefer singles, for which, by the way, there is a supplement of 10 euros per night.'

'I take it you'll be having a single, Syd?' This from Bill, recalling his sleepless night below Scafell when Bert had told him Syd could snore for Wales.

'What makes you say that, Bill?' asked Syd. 'I don't mind sharing.'

'Well Syd, it may be news to you,' replied Bill, 'but you do tend to make a bit of a noise when you're asleep. I wouldn't mind so much if it sounded like Land of my Fathers but frankly, it sounds more like an elephant with toothache.'

Syd said he had no idea he snored as loudly as that. Maybe that was why his wife preferred to sleep in the spare room and yes, he would have a single in the hotel.

'Me too,' said Harry.

When the cries of disbelieve had subsided, O.L., visibly shocked, spluttered out:

'You? You want a single? You mean you're coming with us? To the Alps? In spite of what you said at the last meeting?'

'I am.' replied Harry. 'And if you want to know who to thank for the pleasure of my company, thank Mavis. Very persuasive is Mavis. If you ever get tired of teaching, Mavis, you should take up politics or become an evangelical preacher.'

Bert muttered that if Mavis could convert Harry to walking up mountains, she was definitely wasted as a teacher. Harry nodded at this and went on to say what had made him change his mind: the brilliant photos of the Chamonix valley in the tourist brochures Mavis had shown him, the choice of walks available to a modest walker like himself, the numerous cable cars and chair-lifts that made the walks easily accessible and, not least, the prospect of eating well.

Mavis smiled wryly but made no comment. Harry had conspicuously failed to mention Monique, the real reason for his change of mind. The omission was not lost on his pal Bert either who had known Harry since primary school. Members of the club enjoyed their badinage almost as much as Harry's spats with O.L.

'Nothing to do with the lovely Monique then, Harry, your change of mind? You haven't had a personal invitation from her, by any chance? You'll be able to continue instructing her in the finer arts of photography like you did in Teesdale. And improving her pronunciation of English. As well as practicing all that French you''ve been learning at night school since then.'

'Well, Bert,' replied Harry poker-faced, 'since you mention it, those things did vaguely cross my mind. If the lady in question wishes to take advantage of my expertise in the arts of photography and English pronunciation, it would surely be unchivalrous of me, unkind even, to say her nay, would it not?' You yourself, I seem to recall, chivalrously offered to keep an eye on the lady in my presumed absence.'

Harry had gone into histrionic mode. At his drama club, he was only given bit-parts but here, he was centre stage and he made the most of it. His audience had come to expect performances like this and for the most part, found them highly entertaining. Not so O.L.

'Ladies and gentlemen, if Mr Birch has quite finished his speech, perhaps we can get back to practical matters. About room requirements, we have three people wanting singles – Syd, Mr Birch and myself. I imagine Mavis will share with Betty, Joyce with Penny, Mike with Joe and Bert with Bill. That makes 4 twins.'

Not waiting to hear of any objections, she went on:

'Item 2 on the agenda is our choice of walks. Mavis has shown me the guide-book and map sent by Monique along with a short list of eight walks she personally recommends. What we have to do is choose five of them. The book's in French of course so we'll need Mavis to translate. If Mike, Mavis and I get our heads together, I'm sure we'll be able to come up with a very interesting programme between us.'

Alarm bells rang for Harry but Penny got in first.

'Hold on, Olive. We're not all mountain goats like Mike and you. I'd like to see the walks you propose before I sign up. You know I'm not fond of long, strenuous walks, especially scrambling over rocks.'

Mavis offered reassusance. She wasn't a mountain goat either and nor was Joyce. As for Harry, well they all knew the kind of walks he preferred. She would make sure that everyone was comfortable with the programme they proposed. She herself had done four of the eight walks suggested by Monique and no-one would have a problem with them. Besides, they would use cable-cars whenever possible.'

At this point, Bert burst into life. Thumbing through his Official Guide to Chamonix, he had arrived at the section on cable-cars.

'I don't believe it! Look at page 29. They charge 42.50 euros for a return trip to the *Aiguille du Midi*! I'd sooner walk up!'

'I don't think you would, Bert,' replied Mavis. 'It's at 3,842 metres! Anyway, that would be an option for the free day. You could take Harry to the leisure park instead, if you wanted. They only charge 5.50 for a roller-coaster sledge run that's nearly a mile long. You could afford that, surely.'

Bert said he'd consider it but doubted whether Harry would be interested in sledging on his free day: he'd be too busy sun-bathing by the pool, licking his wounds. Giving Harry no time to respond, Mavis said they would probably be using cable-cars on four days and she would see if buying a multipass would be worthwhile. In any case, walking up, was out of the question. There was, incidentally, a consolation Bert would be pleased to know about. Buses and trains in the Chamonix Valley would cost them nothing! As visitors, they would be given a guest card which also allowed them reductions at museums and the sports centre with its 50 metre open-air swimming pool.

Returning to Penny's doubts about the proposed walks, Harry thought she might like to know more about the balcony paths which had been mentioned. Bert too if they didn't involve paying for cable-cars.

'Well,' said Mavis, 'no problem getting on to the *Petits Balcons*: they are only about 200 metres above the valley floor. But if you want to avoid a climb of about 1000 metres to get on the *Grands Balcons*, you'd have to take a cable-car.'

Mavis was in O.L's black books for two reasons. First and foremost because she had persuaded Harry Birch to change his mind. Secondly, because she had said the group would use cable-cars whenever possible.

'Speaking for myself,' she proclaimed, 'I disapprove of cable-cars. Not, like Bert, because they are expensive but on grounds of principle. I deplore their very existence. They are a blot on the landscape. They bring up hordes of noisy, camera-clicking tourists to desecrate the mountains.. Walkers, real walkers that is, use their legs. I'm sure Mr Wainwright would agree with me. I can't imagine *him* taking short-cuts in a cable-car.'

O.L. had always known there would be problems choosing walks to suit everyone. She had hoped that she and Mike would be able to overrule Mavis and draw up a programme of really challenging walks without relying on cable-cars. Now that Mavis had pre-empted her to win over the weaker members, it was clear that some compromise would have to be made. Smiling sweetly to demonstrate her flexibility, she continued:

'Nevertheless, to accommodate our less energetic members, I'm prepared to make use of these artificial means of ascent and I'm sure, with the benefit of Mavis's knowledge of the terrain, we'll be able to suggest walks within the scope of all of us, We have, after all, several months in which to reach maximum fitness.'

Having reassured Penny and not a few others, O.L. now thought the time was ripe to mention what had been in her mind since first receiving Monique's invitation to Chamonix.

'What particularly interests me, and I think Mike and Joe, is the possibility of climbing Mont-Blanc. From the research: I've done, I gather it's a two day expedition with a night in the *Goûter* refuge. I thought we might use the free day and the next day .... if you can do without us, that is.'

Harry was the first to put her mind at rest.

'Speaking as one of the less energetic members, I think I can safely say there would certainly be no objection on that score. But aren't you being just a bit too ambitious, Olive? Nobody doubts your determination but, let's face it, you're well over 70.'

Hating to be reminded of her age, O.L. retorted sharply:

'Touched as I am by your concern, Mr Birch, I think I am as fit or fitter than many people half my age. I'll be running a half marathon in May. Perhaps you'd care to join me?'

'Never do things by halves, Olive,' came Harry's reply. 'All or nothing, that's me but thanks all the same for the thought.'

Mike and Joe also had reservations about O.L. Still, climbing Mont-Blanc was high on their own wish list and they were willing to give her the benefit of the doubt providing she understood exactly what was involved..

'It's no picnic, you know, Olive.' said Mike, 'We can get part way up by cable car and mountain railway but from the *Nid d'Aigle* up to the *Goûter* hut there's nearly 1500 metres of climbing. And almost 1000 metres next day to the summit.'

'Not to mention the descent,' added Joe. 'After four hours climbing in snow to the top, we'd then have a descent of 2500 metres to reach the railway. Think about it, Olive.'

'We'd need to hire a professional guide, of course,' went on Mike. 'Ever worn crampons, used an ice-axe or been roped up, Olive?'

'No I haven't,' O.L. replied briskly, 'and if you think you're putting me off, you can think again. I've plenty of time to learn about crampons, ice-axes and ropes. I'm sure you two would make excellent teachers. I realise we'd need a guide, of course, but I should think Monique will be able to find one for us. That's settled then: I'll give Monique the dates we have in mind and ask her to find us a guide, preferably with at least a smattering of English.'

No-one could accuse O.L. of shilly-shallying! Some members appreciated what they called her 'decisive leadership.' Others, notably Harry, saw her as a petty dictator, bulldozing over anything or anyone who got in her way. Much too laidback and flippant for O.L.'s taste, Harry frequently got in her way whenever the chance arose, as it now did.

'I'm sure we wish all three of you well, climbing Mont-Blanc but aren't you cheating just a bit? I mean, taking a cable-car and mountain railway part way sounds like a short cut to me. I doubt if Mr Wainwright would approve. After all, don't real walkers use their legs?'

On the defensive, O.L. was forced to concede that perhaps she had been too critical of cable-cars in general. Most were undoubtedly eye-sores and unnecessary but there were exceptions. Given time, she would have been quite willing to set off on foot but that would have added another two days to the climb. Anyway, as far as the programme of walks was concerned, if the group wanted to save their legs by using cable-cars, she had no objection.'

'Happy now, Harry?' called Bert. 'Think you'll be O.K. in those contraptions? Enjoy dangling in mid air, will you? Don't suffer from vertigo, do you?'

'I don't, Bert,' came the reply, 'but you needn't worry about me. You'll have enough to worry about at the turnstiles when you've got to shell out all that brass.'

Before closing the meeting, O.L. said that she would convey their thanks to Monique, send her their choice of walks, ask her to find a guide for Mont Blanc and let her know how many rooms they would take.

'Don't forget to ask for a ground floor room for Harry,' piped up Bert. 'He'll need all the help he can get. After climbing up mountains, he won't want to be climbing up stairs.'

HARRY RE-INVENTS HIMSELF

Harry was beginning to get tired of Bert's jokes at his expense. Mavis too had begun to make remarks about his fitness or lack of it. He expected such comments from O.L. in response to his criticism of her but Bert and he were old pals and Mavis one of his fan club. Bert's parting shot at the last meeting about his need for a ground-floor room had not amused him. Usually he enjoyed their light-hearted banter but this was going too far. He could take a joke as well as make one but being cast as the club's deadleg was beginning to irritate him.

Harry realised he had no-one to blame but himself for this state of affairs. By setting himself up as an antidote to O.L.'s militant leadership, he had adopted the opposite rôle of conscientious objector. If she was humourless, he would be flippant: if she was up-tight, he would be laid-back: if she strode ahead, he would lag behind. Little wonder that now some members of the club saw him as a layabout, a playboy, a butt for their jokes. The last straw was the e-mail he received a week later from Monique.

'Mon cher Harry,

Mavis has told me that you will come to Chamonix next year. I am very pleased. I was not sure you would come. In Teesdale, during our walk, Mavis told me something bizarre: you think your president is a dragon and she thinks you a wimp. What that word signified, I did not know. Now I have found it in my dictionary and I am sure it is not true. It was a joke, was it not? English humour is so difficult for me.

I also received a letter from Mrs Jonstone. She sent me the walks you propose. They are very good. Certainly they will give you pleasure. and you will take some lovely photos. You will help me to perfect my English, will you not? And me, your French.

Your president wants to climb the Mont-Blanc with Mike and Joe!

I must find them a guide. She is very courageous, is she not?

Amitiés,

Monique'

Harry was very pleased to receive an e-mail from Monique but the word wimp upset him. Not that O.L.'s opinion bothered him but maybe she wasn't alone, maybe other members of the club also saw him as a wimp. By appearing everything that O.L. was not, maybe he himself had cultivated this view. Maybe his tactics were flawed. He didn't *have* to appear a wimp in order to rein in O.L Perhaps it was time to change his image.

It was an advert in the local paper that galvanised Harry into action. "To improve your health, your stamina and your quality of life, you need a Personal Trainer" ran the headline. Below was a photo of a smiling, bronzed, good-looking, well-built young man, his arm round a smiling, bronzed, good-looking, well-built young woman. At the bottom was a web site which Harry wasted no time in visiting.

The more he read, the more interested he became. Technical terms like 'basal metabolic rate' and 'cardiovascular excercise' meant nothing to him but he did understand, vaguely, that burning off 2000 calories was like burning off a Mars bar. Did that mean he could continue enjoying his daily Mars bar provided he lost 2000 calories? Anyway, if his diet had to be changed, it would be a small price to pay to lose some of the flab round his middle.

Harry was well aware that getting back into shape would involve more than just a change of diet. He had never been near a gym since leaving school but he had seen pictures of people walking briskly on treadmills, pedalling furiously on bicycles, sweating profusely on rowing machines and straining grimly to lift weights. Would a Personal Trainer have him doing likewise? The thought horrified him. He'd hated gym at school. Having to climb ropes, jump over boxes and hang upside down on parallel bars had been bad enough but those so-called fitness machines in gyms smelling of sweat and liniment, looked even worse.

Harry was on the point of abandoning the whole idea when he caught sight of a paragraph headed 'You don't have to come to me: I'll come to YOU.' Reading on eagerly, he discovered that Bernard who called himself an Advanced Personal Trainer and had a diploma to prove it, offered home visits at times convenient to clients. Harry's interest was rekindled at a stroke. No sweaty gym. None of those fiendish machines. The comfort of his own home. At times of his choosing. Brilliant!

Further down the page, he read the testimonials. One man claimed to have lost 2½ stones in three months! Another said he'd lost 1 stone over a similar period. Both maintained they had actually enjoyed their sessions with Bernard. Even more inspiring were some before-and-after photos of clients who had been miraculously rejuvenated. After losing weight, they not only looked better but claimed they felt better about themselves and had much more energy. Reading all this strengthened Harry's motivation. The fact that home visits cost more than if he went to a gym was unimportant. Bernard even guaranteed results after six weeks! Harry picked up the phone and made an appointment in two days' time.

It was all very professional. After a series of tests to show heart rate, blood pressure, strength, percentage of body fat and muscle, Harry was asked numerous questions about his objectives, his life style, his diet and his alcohol consumption. Bernard frowned at some of his answers and finally said, only half jokingly, that he enjoyed a challenge. He suggested two hour-long sessions a week and when Mondays and Thursdays from 9 a.m. to 10 had been agreed upon, Harry left, feeling well satisfied. He would make O.L. eat her words. Neither she nor anyone else in the club was now going to see him as a wimp. He might, eventually, mention having a Personal Trainer but for the time being, he would keep quiet about it. It would be amusing to see O.L.'s reaction when he had slimmed down and put a spring in his step. There would be no more jibes from Bert: what's more, Monique would be impressed!

When Bernard arrived for Harry's first session, he started off by saying that there were only two ways of losing weight, cutting down on carbohydrates and taking exercise. First, he would deal with carbs. Harry was then handed a list of food and drinks to be avoided if he wanted to lose his middle-age spread. He'd have to steer clear of cakes, biscuits, crisps, sweets and chocolate. Fast food such as burgers were a no-no as were fatty foods such as soft cheese. The ban on fizzy drinks didn't bother Harry at all: what did bother him very much was learning that alcohol produced nearly as many calories as fat.

It was obvious that sacrifices would have to be made. He would miss his Mars bars, cream sponges and camembert but, worst of all, he'd have to cut down drastically on Guinness, his favourite tipple. He would also have to develop a taste for food he rarely bought: whole grain bread, brown rice and pasta along with fruit and vegetables.

Cutting down on carbohydrates wasn't the only thing he had to do. For a balanced diet, his protein level had to be maintained. This he should do by eating chicken breast, lean beef or pork, fish, preferably oily fish, and eggs. He should also drink plenty of water, ideally two litres a day. Harry uttered a sigh of relief: these were foods he knew and enjoyed. The only problem would be drinking so much water. Up to now, he'd only drunk water when Guinness was not available.

Bernard now spoke about the second way to lose weight, exercise, which was simply a way of burning off calories. Apparently, cardiovascular exercises, working on the heart and lungs, were the most effective way of doing this. Strength training by means of weight lifting was also useful in burning calories as well as improving muscle tone. Here Bernard felt obliged to point out that although converting fat into muscle was *a very good thing*, muscle weighed more than fat, so he shouldn't be alarmed if there was no immediate loss of weight.

Harry was impatient to get started. He had bought a tracksuit, his first ever, and a pair of state-of-the-art trainers but not at the outdoor shop where Joyce worked – she would have spread the news round the club like wildfire. Now wearing only shorts and vest, he began a series of warm-ups following his trainer's instructions to the letter. As more strenuous exercises were introduced, his joints began to creak in protest, his breath became more laboured and perspiration trickled down his nose. Pleased with his efforts, Bernard encouraged him to persevere: there was no gain without pain. It was only when Harry collapsed in a heap, panting, that a halt was called and a glass of water suggested.

While he was recovering, Bernard went out to his van and came back with a punchball and some weights. Now was the time to start muscle toning. Harry's long dormant muscles had already been rudely awakened and he wasn't at all keen to have them 'toned' whatever that meant. He was soon to find out. Punching the ball and lifting the weights brought to life muscles which he never knew existed. His whole body ached, he was sweating profusely and he was breathless. Bernard said he was doing fine and now they would do some breathing exercises to finish, after which he should take a shower and have a good rub down. Before leaving, he gave Harry the lists of prohibited and recommended foods together with a sheaf of papers illustrating the excercises done that morning which he should practise every day. He also advocated jogging, interspersed with power walking. To begin with, a mile would be far enough but he should increase the distance little by little as his fitness improved.

The unaccustomed exertion plus all the advice he had been given left Harry physically and mentally drained. What he needed now was not a shower but a long hot bath in which to soak his aching limbs and reflect on his morning's work-out. It hadn't been easy and he clearly had a long way to go but at least he'd made a start. If anything, he was more determined then ever to achieve the goal he had set himself. Emerging from his bath, he made up his mind to set the alarm next day for 7 and start jogging at 8. There wouldn't be many people about at that time so there was less chance of bumping into anyone who might recognise him.

When the alarm woke him at 7, Harry groaned as he remembered his resolve to go jogging but forced himself to crawl out of bed. Dressed in his new tracksuit and trainers, he made porridge, toasted a slice of whole-grain bread and ate an apple, contenting himself with two glasses of water, before setting off for the park. To his relief – he didn't want an audience on his first outing – the only other people in sight were two men walking their dogs. The last time he'd done any running was three years ago trying to catch a bus: he remembered collapsing exhausted onto a wall after twenty yards.

It wasn't easy to develop a rhythm. His legs were stiff after yesterday's exercises and an ungainly shuffle was all he could manage for the first fifty yards. Pausing to get his breath back, he decided a spell of brisk walking might loosen him up. Brisk was not the word O.L. would have used but she would have acknowledged an improvement on his usual saunter. Alternating between running and walking, he completed the circuit of the park in 20 minutes before sinking onto a bench. To his surprise, he felt quite refreshed after a few minutes rest. and after some deep breathing exercises, felt sufficiently energised to set off again.

Twice round the park in 40 minutes! As he slowly made his way home, Harry felt a huge sense of achievement. He had done what no-one, himself included, would have thought conceivable a few days ago. If he could stick to his new diet regime, do the exercises as prescribed and continue jogging every day, he'd be as fit as a butcher's dog in next to no time. Any more snide remarks from Bert and he'd challenge him to a race. If O.L. queried his ability to get up Pen-y-Ghent on their next outing, he'd get there before her. He couldn't wait to see how surprised they'd be.

It was when passing the school where Mavis taught that he caught sight of a familiar figure coming towards him. He would normally have been pleased to bump into Mavis but not today, dressed as he was. He ducked into the nearest doorway, hoping he hadn't been recognised, annoyed at not having thought of the possibility of meeting Mavis on her way to school. When she sailed past him, he heaved a sigh of relief and was about to emerge when he realised he'd ducked into the doorway of the library where Penny worked. Rushing out of the library, Penny exclaimed:

'Harry Birch, at this time of morning! And wearing a track suit! I don't believe it! You've never been running, have you? You look flushed and you smell sweaty.'

Unable to bluff his way out, Harry had to find some way to account for his appearance but decided there was no need to tell her the full story: he would keep quiet about having acquired a personal trainer.

'Well, Penny,' he began nonchalantly, 'as a matter of fact, I've just been for a little canter round the park. Felt like stretching my legs. I can recommend it. Why don't you join me some time? I'd appreciate your company.'

Penny seemed to accept this explanation although she confessed to being very surprised saying she didn't think he had it in him. As for joining him, jogging wasn't really her scene but she would think about it.

Harry was about to leave when he appeared to think of something he'd forgotten. Would she do him a favour and not mention having seen him in a tracksuit and trainers. It would be blown up out of all proportion by Bert and he could do without the aggro. If she were to join him occasionally, nobody need know about that either. It would be their little secret. Penny nodded in agreement and Harry left, thinking he'd saved the day.

O.L.'S AMAZEMENT

At the next fortnightly meeting at the Rose and Crown, when Harry made an entrance, Guinness in hand, Bert immediately noticed something odd.

'What's up Harry?' he asked. 'Never seen you drinking halves before. Feeling under the weather, are you? You haven't joined Weight Watchers, by any chance?'

'No to both questions, Bert. As a matter of fact, I've never felt better,' replied Harry, without giving any further explanation.

Business-like as usual, O.L. called the meeting to order. First on the agenda was the letter she had just received from Monique about climbing Mont Blanc. She had been rather disconcerted to learn that the ratio of guides to clients was 1:2 so two guides not one would be needed for Mike, Joe and herself. Moreover, an extra day would be needed to demonstrate their fitness, wearing crampons and using ice-axes prior to the climb. The total cost, including transport, accommodation in the *Goûter* hut and hiring two guides could amount to about £1000 each.

'Out of the question, Olive,' was Mike's immediate response. 'Couldn't afford it.'

'Same here,' said Joe. 'If my wife knew I was spending that much to get up Mont Blanc, my life wouldn't be worth living.'

O.L. was not surprised by their reactions. She herself had been dismayed by the cost although she would have shrugged it off. What concerned her, was demonstrating her technique wearing crampons and using an ice-axe. Would some super fit young guide have her leaping over crevasses and burying her ice-axe into walls of frozen snow? What if he rejected her as too old or not fit enough! Maybe she had been too ambitious after all.

'I understand how you feel,' she told Mike and Joe. 'Apart from the cost, we'd be away from the group for three days, not two. Then there's the possibility of having to abort because of bad weather. Very well, I'll let Monique know we've had second thoughts.'

'I'm sure that's the right thing to do,' said Harry gravely. 'We don't want to be pushing our luck at our time of life, do we?'

Ignoring this remark, O.L. went on to talk about travel arrangements. She had learned of a flight from Liverpool arriving in Geneva at 16.25. A hired minibus from there would get them to their hotel about 6 p.m. After a good night's sleep, they would all feel fighting fit for their first walk in the mountains next morning.

'Nothing too strenuous, I hope,' cried Penny.

'You don't need worry about that, Penny. We've made allowances for our less ambitious members. Now, to return to the subject of travel, would Mr Birch be kind enough to book flghts and minibus? I'm sure he'd have no difficulty doing this on his computer.'

This request took Harry by surprise. As president, O.L. normally undertook such responsabilities herself: they came with the job. In her eyes, delegating them to someone else was a sign of weakness and a dereliction of duty. Harry slowly got to his feet. Centre stage, he bowed in acknowledgement.

'Nothing would give me greater pleasure, Olive. Rest assured, all will be well. An itinerary will be printed out and given to each and everyone concerned. At our next meeting, I will inform you of the total cost. You can pay me by cheque or folding money as you wish. And no, Bert, before you ask, small change from your piggy bank will not be acceptable.'

Leaving Bert no time to reply, O.L. thanked Harry and went on to say how much she was looking forward to Sunday's walk up Pen-y-Ghent in the Yorkshire Dales, led by ex-army sergeant, Bill. With a bit of luck there might be a sprinkling of snow on the summit. It was only 693 metres high and involved only 450 metres of climbing from Horton but they should think of it as the first of their training walks. She would have more to say about the others she was planning in the new year.

Gladys, the peace-maker, respected O.L. and also had a soft spot for Harry. So far, neither had provoked the other: they had even shown a willingness to co-operate. At this point, she feared Harry would make some withering remark about O.L.'s wish for snow and her twice repeated 'only' to play down the amount of climbing. She was pleased when Harry merely voiced the opinion that a training walk eight months before departure was a little premature although he supposed it would do them no harm to give their legs a stretch.

O.L. raised an eyebrow at this before Bill broke in to describe the route he was proposing. The southern side of Pen-y-Ghent was steep and rocky, easier to climb than descend especially if there was a covering of snow. They would go up via Brackenbottom, meet the Pennine Way and follow it up to the summit and back down to Horton. Walking poles would be useful if the ground was slippery.

Bert now saw an opportunity to level the score after Harry's remark about his piggy bank.

'You might have trouble with your zimmer frame on those rocks, Harry. You wouldn't want us calling up Mountain Rescue, would you. I can just see the headlines: 'Walker on zimmer frame air-lifted from peak.' You'd be on all the front pages.'

Strangely enough, Harry appeared to find this almost as amusing as O.L. In fact, what he really found amusing was the prospect of making Bert eat his words. After religiously doing the exercises prescribed, regular jogging in the park, healthy eating and cutting down his consumption of Guinness, Harry had slimmed substantially and felt fitter than he'd felt for years. Penny too, claimed to be in better shape. After jogging with Harry three times a week she had finally acquired a rhythm which didn't leave her panting. Both were looking forward to the climb up Pen-y-Ghent as a test of their progress.

When compiling the winter programme, O.L. had thought Bill was being optimistic in proposing to climb Pen-y-Ghent. Even in summer, its summit was often shrouded in cloud: in January, it could also be covered with snow. Naturally enough, she had not expressed any reservations at the time. She herself would enjoy battling against the elements and she'd certainly not shed any tears if fine weather walkers like Harry Birch opted to stay at home. Having to wait for stragglers was one of her pet hates.

Now that the day had come, with rain and sleet beating against the car windows as she drove to the rendezvous, she wondered who would turn out on such a morning. Not Harry, Joyce, Gladys and Penny for sure, she would bet her life on that. It was just as well that O.L. was not a gambler. Pulling in to the car park, she saw, in stunned disbelief, a red, two-seater. sports car from which Harry and Penny were just emerging.

'Morning, Olive,' cried Harry, 'I won't say *good* morning given the weather but come to think about it, you must be pleased. You were hoping for snow, weren't you? If there's sleet down here, there's sure to be snow on Pen-y-Ghent.'

O.L. managed a weak smile, expressed surprise at seeing Harry and said yes, she had hoped for snow. Looking round, she assessed the turn-out: there were four strong walkers, Bill, Mike, Joe and herself; two she considered average, Bert and Mavis and the two unexpected plodders, Harry and Penny. At least her friend Gladys had wisely opted out: she would have been slithering all over the place. Of the 11 going to Chamonix, Syd, Joyce and Betty were missing. When Bill said he was pleasantly surprised by the turn-out, O.L. didn't say 'me too.' Surprised, certainly but pleasantly surprised, no. She was afraid they might have problems with Harry and Penny.

As expected, there was a light covering of snow at Horton and the summit of Pen-y-Ghent was in cloud. Bill recommended putting on over-trousers straight away. He was pleased that no-one was wearing a cape – it would be windy higher up where capes would be useless – and that everyone except O.L. and Bert had followed his advice and brought a stick or poles To Bert, these were an unnecessary expense; to O.L., they were just unnecessary. Both were to have second thoughts later in the day.

As they left the car park, it was Bill, not Harry, who suggested calling at the café for a hot chocolate and a warm-up before setting off. Predictably, O.L. was not in favour of stopping before they'd started. What *was* surprising was seeing Harry hesitate: he seemed to be debating whether to go in with the others or not. After a few seconds, he joined them and ordered a hot chocolate without sugar. He'd kept off chocolate in any shape or form with great difficulty up to now but today, the weather being what it was, he felt justified in making an exception.

'Had me worried there, Harry,' called out Bert. 'Thought you must be sickening for something. This chocolate should set you up for a mile or two. Not sure how you'll get on after that. Haven't forgotten your Mars bars, I hope.'

'Actually, my old fruit, I've given them up,' replied Harry smiling. 'I'm relying on nuts and bananas. When you're rolling about in the snow up there without poles, I'll give you some. They might get you on your feet again.'

Bill broke in to say they had a steady climb of 350 metres over about two miles to reach the Pennine Way at the foot of Pen-y-Ghent. If, as he expected, visibility became poor as they gained height, they should keep within three or four yards of each other.

Snow was dancing in the air as they came out of the café and joined the track to Brackenbottom led by O.L. and Mike with Harry in his usual position at the tail-end alongside Penny. Behind them came Joe who had agreed to be back-marker. There were no steep gradients on the stony track but having to negotiate patches of ice, often disguised by a layer of snow, made progress slow as did the squally showers driven into their faces by a freshening east wind.

'It was never like this, jogging round the park, Harry,' gasped Penny. 'Do you think we'll make it to the top?'

'Can't think why not, Penny. We haven't done all that fitness training for nothing. Just keep up a steady pace and control your breathing. If you start flagging, have some of those nuts and raisins I gave you.'

Harry himself felt fine. Keeping to his plan of campaign, he had started off at the back. Now, after twenty minutes, he began to quicken his pace leaving Penny with Joe in order to catch up with Bert and Mavis. Harry didn't need to go on tiptoe to surprise them: his footsteps were muffled by three inches of snow.

'Bless my soul, it's Harry Birch, the Abominable Snowman himself,' cried Bert, 'with two poles and a spring in his step. What did you have for breakfast, Harry?'

'A large bowl of porridge laced with honey followed by two slices of toast thickly coated with marmalde,' replied Harry, 'followed by a banana, all washed down with two glasses of apple juice. I can recommend it.'

'If that's what it does for you, I might even give it a try,' exclaimed Bert.

As Harry lengthened his stride to catch up with Bill, Mike and O.L., Mavis suspected that a change of diet couldn't by itself account for Harry's s new-found surge of energy. He had obviously lost weight but there had to be another explanation. She would find out sooner or later. As to what had motivated him, of that she had no doubt. It was obviously to make a good impression on Monique in Chamonix.

As Harry strode ahead, Bert couldn't believe what he was seeing. Harry among the leaders, walking briskly uphill against driving snow? It couldn't last: he was just trying to score a point. He would soon burn himself out and be straggling behind as usual.

Bert's disbelief was shared by O.L. when Harry drew level with her.

'Harry Birch,' she spluttered. 'I don't believe it! It's not your twin brother, is it?'

Harry informed her curtly that he didn't have a twin brother and she didn't have to look as if she'd seen a ghost. He could walk as well as anyone if he felt so inclined.

When they reached the Pennine Way signpost, Bill decided it was time to picnic. A wall offered some protection from the blustery wind and Harry took it upon himself to trample down the soft snow which had drifted against it.

'Make yourselves at home, ladies and gentlemen,' he cried in his stage voice. 'You probably wish you were there. Admittedly, the dining room's a tad draughty but at least you've got a back-rest against this wall. My good friend Bert and I would have built an igloo if he hadn't taken so long getting here. I can only imagine he's saving his energy for the climb to the summit. If I'd brought my zimmer frame, Bert, I'd have lent it to you. Failing which, allow me to offer you one of my poles.'

Bert was just about to tell Harry where he could stick his pole but thought better of it. Instead, he muttered something about there being a long way to go yet and doubted if Harry would make it even with his two poles. O.L. took a similar view. It was too early to express her relief at not being kept waiting by Harry but she did have a word of praise for Penny who had kept up a steady pace with Joe and showed no undue signs of fatigue.

Bill didn't want to linger over the picnic. There were already four inches of snow underfoot and there would be more on the top. Great care would be needed on the rocky ascent: they should follow him in single file, not stray from the path and keep within three yards of each other. They would meet the cloud base halfway up and poor visibility could make things tricky. At least they wouldn't have the wind in their faces but a gusty side wind could throw them off balance if they weren't very careful.

Harry positioned himself behind the leading trio of Bill, Mike and O.L. as the path steepened and the climb began. There was frozen snow and ice on the rocks and Bill went slowly to make sure everyone kept together. Harry found his poles helpful in keeping his balance on the treacherous surface and quietly enjoyed the sight of O.L. floundering and, at times, having to use her hands. He toyed with the idea of overtaking her but as Bill had said single file, that pleasure would have to be deferred. Coming up behind him, Bert was also struggling to stay upright. Once, when his feet slid from under him, he had to be helped up by Harry, luckily suffering nothing worse than dented pride.

Bill counted his flock as they loomed out of the mist and reached level ground on the summit. He had told them that Pen-y-Ghent meant 'hill of the winds' and now they knew why. With a blizzard howling round them, climbing the stile to get on the leeward side of the wall was in itself fraught with risk. Penny wobbled alarmingly on the top rung and it needed the combined efforts of Bill and Mike to bring her down to ground level. Getting everyone safely over was a slow process. Waiting their turn to cross, Mavis, Harry and Joe stamped their feet and rubbed their hands together. On the other side, Bert was massaging his legs and O.L. was running on the spot. It was no place to hang about.

When they were all huddled together, Bill had a word of warning. Although the descent was not as steep or rocky as the way they had come up, more care was needed, not less. A slip going downhill could have serious consequences. To make a controlled descent, they should use their poles as brakes. At this point, remembering that neither Bert nor O.L. had brought poles, Bill insisted on giving one of his own to O.L. and asked Mike to give one of his to Bert. Still shaken by his fall, Bert showed no reluctance to accept Mike's pole but O.L. at first declined until Bill pointed out that if she were to have an accident, she wouldn't be the only one to suffer, the whole group would be affected. Finally she condescended to accept

Bill's pole as if she were doing everyone a favour.

The beginning of the descent in six inches of snow wasn't made any easier by the strong side wind but when they turned west, with the wind in their backs, making a slow, controlled descent was not easy. O.L. in particular, even with Bill's pole, was having trouble staying upright.

Up to this point, Harry was well pleased with his performance: he had already succeeded in demonstrating his newly found fitness to Bert and O.L. but now the strain was starting to tell. Having to brake at each step made his knees feel weak. When they suddenly gave way, he found himself on his back careering towards O.L. His warning shout came too late for her to get out of his way. Bill managed to bring them to a stop by throwing himself on O.L. but both she and Harry were badly shaken. Bert's remark that they looked like a two-man bob sleigh on the Cresta run failed to amuse them; it could have been disastrous. Harry apologised profusely. To his surprise, O.L. shrugged off his apologies: a slip like that could have happened to any of them, herself included. They should take it as a warning and be ultra careful from now on.

As the gradient eased, they reached a wall where Bill called a halt. O.L. passed round a bar of chocolate which Harry had no qualms in accepting. He, in turn, distributed nuts and raisins and presented bananas to Penny and Bert. There were still flurries of snow in the air but the visibility had improved and Bill said the worst was over, they would be down in Horton in about an hour. All the same, care was still needed: there was plenty of snow and ice on the track and they were all, to a greater or lesser extent, suffering from fatigue. He would set the pace and he didn't want anyone overtaking him.

Harry had envisaged speeding up on the last lap to overtake Bert and O.L. but now he'd have to keep in line. In a way, he was relieved. His knees still felt weak and if they were to let him down again, it would look like burn-out. Feeling he had already done enough to confound his critics, Harry abandoned his idea of a triumphal last lap and decided to walk down wih Mavis who at last had the chance to satisfy her curiosity.

'Well Harry,' she began, 'you've certainly raised a few eyebrows today. What's the magic formula for your transformation? Don't tell me it's all down to a change of diet.'

'No Mavis, there's a lot more to it than that. But you'll have to promise to keep quiet about it. My transformation as you put it, is a work in progress and I don't want the others to know how I've done it until it's complete.'

When Mavis said her lips were sealed, Harry went on to describe the twice weekly visits of Bernard his personal trainer, the muscle toning exercises he'd been doing religiously every day as well as an hour's jogging round the park three times a week. To get rid of flab, he'd been following the diet recommended by Bernard and cut down his consumption of alcohol by more than a half.

'Well I must say I'm impressed, Harry,' exclaimed Mavis. 'I wouldn't have thought it possible. I admire your determination. It can't have been easy.'

'Easy it wasn't, Mavis. For the first week I was aching all over. You could say it's been a triumph of mind over matter. My form today has made all that pain and sweat seem worthwhile. But I've still got work to do. When I sent O.L. sprawling on that steep slope, my knees just gave way and they still feel weak. I'll have a word with Bernard about that tomorrow.'

There were no more mishaps before they got down to Horton and this time, Harry did not hesitate when they arrived at the café. No need to feel guilty about his second hot chocolate of the day – it had been well earned – but he resisted the temptation to indulge in the cream sponge that Bert offered him by way of congratulation, claiming that nuts and raisins were more nutricious. Never before had Bert known Harry refuse a cream sponge, show the slightest interest in nuts and raisins and drink chocolate without sugar. Nor could he remember a time when Harry had walked so briskly and kept pace with the leaders.

'I must admit, Harry,' he exclaimed, 'you've done exceptionally well today. How, I can't imagine. You haven't been popping pills by any chance as well as nuts and raisins? I think you should be dope tested like they do with cyclists on the Tour de France.'

'Nothing to do with drugs, Bert,' replied Harry smiling, 'Put it down to will-power. And by the way, regarding that zimmer frame you mentioned, it's up for sale: no reasonable offer refused. If you care to make a bid, I can assure you it will receive my fullest consideration.'

Bert grinned. Harry had levelled the score. It was now O.L.'s turn to make her customary speech at the end of a walk.

'Ladies and gentlemen,' she began, in Captain

Mainwaring mode, 'we have just finished a walk which, by any standards, could be described as taxing. We have climbed 450 metres over rough and rocky terrain in driving snow and gale force winds to reach our goal. Even more difficult, treacherous even, was our descent in deep snow lying on a bed of ice. I think we can all take pride in having braved the elements on our walk today and I'm sure you would wish me to express our thanks to Bill for his advice and decisive leadership.'

'And to him and Mike for lending you and Bert one of their poles.' added Harry mischievously. 'I imagine you'll both be investing in a pair before we go to Chamonix.'

'I must admit, Harry,' replied O.L., 'I did find that pole useful on the descent. As for investing in a pair, I remain to be convinced. Let me remind you that your two poles didn't prevent you from losing control and crashing into me. In spite of that lapse, however, I feel obliged to say how impressed I have been by your overall performance today. Whether you can maintain such form on future walks remains to be seen. If so, your earlier reservations about walking in Chamonix will prove groundless.'

'Harry for Mont-Blanc!' cried Bert. 'I can just see him on the top with his two poles, chewing nuts and raisins, planting the Union Jack in the snow, monarch of all he surveys.'

Bert was obviously taking the mickey but Harry took it as a compliment. Before today's walk, the very idea of him climbing Mont-Blanc would have been inconceivable. Even O.L. now had an uncomfortable feeling that it was not totally beyond the bounds of possibility. On today's showing, she considered his transformation from tortoise to hare nothing short of a miracle.

Driving home, Harry reviewed the day's events with satisfaction. He had put Bert in his place and amazed O.L. Mission accomplished.

COUNTDOWN

O.L. had ear-marked the last three Sundays before their departure for Chamonix as what she termed 'training walks.' Asked by Harry what she had in mind, she announced that after careful consideration she'd decided on Skiddaw, Helvellyn and Scafell Pike, three of the four highest mountains in England. They would be excellent preparation for getting the most out of their walks in the Alps. She was sure everyone would agree.

Gladys held her breath. Not so very long ago, Harry would have objected immediately to O.L.'s automatic assumption that everyone agreed with her. He would have pointed out that he himself, and he wasn't the only one, had no desire to risk life and limb sweating up the highest mountains in England prior to departure. It was quite unnecessary. They would have enough sweating to do when they got to Chamonix. They weren't all masochists.

In the event, Gladys need not have worried that hostilities were about to break out. Harry held his peace and it was left to Joyce to express concern. Recalling her accident below Scafell a year ago and being air-lifted off to hospital, she said she wouldn't feel comfortable on Helvellyn judging from the photos she'd seen of Striding Edge and Swirral Edge. Nor did she fancy picking her way over the boulder field below Scafell Pike. It would be better for all concerned if she didn't tempt fate.

When Penny said she too had similar reservations, Gladys suggested that the three of them might do less taxing walks on the lower slopes of Helvellyn and Scafell Pike.

'No problem there,' interposed Mike. 'You could go with us from Glenridding as far as the Hole in the Wall and return via Lanty's Tarn. You'd still have a climb of about 500 metres but you wouldn't have to face Striding Edge.'

'No problem either when we go to Scafell Pike,' added Joe. 'You could go up Grains Gill with us from Seathwaite as far as Sprinkling Tarn and return via Sty Head and Stockley Bridge. We could all meet up in the farmhouse café.'

Much relieved at not being lumbered with Gladys, Penny and Joyce on Helvellyn and Scafell Pike, O.L. said that climbing Skiddaw presented no difficulty. She proposed taking Mr Wainwright's preferred route from Ravenstone over Ullock Pike. The only problem for the three ladies might be the climb of 830 metres but, if they didn't feel up to it, they could call a halt after 500 metres when they got to Ullock Pike and go down by the same way.

At this point, not so very long ago, Bert would have chipped in to say that Harry would no doubt be delighted to escort the ladies down from Ullock Pike if, that is, he ever got there. Bert didn't chip in. He knew very well that on current form, Harry would reach the summit of Skiddaw, let alone Ullock Fell. The three high-level training walks proposed by O.L. would prove beyond dispute his staying power.

After Bernard's twice weekly visits over a period of three months, Harry thought a personal trainer was no longer necessary. Bernard agreed but warned him against slipping back into his bad old ways. He should continue the muscle-toning exercises, regular jogging and above all, keep strictly to the diet regime he'd been recommended. Harry needed no convincing. He had lost nearly two stones, felt better and looked better. He actually enjoyed his early morning jogs round the park, especially with Penny.

It was on one of his solo runs that he suddenly became aware of another jogger rapidly closing in on him.

'Morning,' he called out as he was overtaken. 'Morning,' came a shrill voice in reply. Both stopped abruptly.

'Harry Birch!,' spluttered O.L. 'I can't believe it. What are you doing here?'

'Much the same as yourself, I imagine, Olive, enjoying a little run round the park. Helps to keep the flab down. Got to be in good form for Chamonix.'

'So this is how you amazed us all on Pen-y-Ghent! Jogging round the park.'

'Well, there's a little more to it than that,' went on Harry casually. 'A change of diet helped. And a few knees-up made a difference.'

Harry knew he had been rumbled but he saw no need to go into detail, least of all to mention his personal trainer.

'A difference? A transformation more like it!' cried O.L. 'I think congratulations are in order. If you change your mind about the half marathon I'm training for, let me know. Must be off now. I've another ten laps to do.'

Harry had no intention of running a half marathon but he couldn't help admiring O.L.'s determination. Well over 70, she refused to make any concessions to her age. True, she was intolerant of others who lacked her strength of purpose but maybe he had been too harsh in his judgment of her. Whatever her faults, she certainly commanded respect.

Harry's newly found respect for O.L. was mutual. Since Pen-y-Ghent, her opinion of him had risen from rock bottom to near admiration. On subsequent Sunday walks, admittedly in better weather and over easier terrain, he had shown no signs of flagging. It was the chance meeting in the park that made her realise how much effort and will-power must have gone into his transformation. She would still disapprove of his flamboyant appearance and his attention-seeking histrionics – a far cry from her rôle model, Mr Wainwright – but she could no longer dismiss Harry Birch as a playboy lacking moral fibre.

When she proposed 7 a.m. starts for the training walk to the Lakes, it was Bert who grumbled not Harry. To allow him plenty of time for his customary breakfast fry-ups, Harry offered to give him a wake-up call at 6 but was told bluntly not to bother. Also curtly rejected was his offer of nuts and raisins if Bert got up too late for his bacon and eggs.

On the climb to Ullock Pike, Harry made a point of walking with Penny, Joyce and Gladys at the back of the group.

'You don't have to walk at our pace, you know Harry,' said Gladys as the gap between themselves and the leaders became wider and wider. 'I don't think Olive is too pleased: she keeps looking back at us.'

'Olive will just have to wait then, won't she,' replied Harry. 'High time she learned some patience. She forgets we're not all as driven as she is.'

'Feeling the strain, are you Harry?' asked Bert grinning when they finally arrived at the parting of the ways on the top of Ullock Pike. 'Run out of nuts and raisins, have you?'

'Never felt better, Bert, and don't worry,' retorted Harry. 'I've plenty of nuts and raisins for both of us. I see you've splashed out on a stick at last – or have you borrowed it?'

Bert's reply was drowned by O.L. announcing picnic time. According to her mentor Mr. Wainwright all worldly troubles vanished on the top of Ullock Pike. He thought it was a delectable spot, a place to linger amongst comfortable heather couches and enjoy magnificent views. She was sure everyone would concur.

It was a more leisurely picnic than usual. Any worldly troubles they may have had soon vanished as they sprawled out in the springy heather in the warmth of the sun. It was only Syd's snoring that got everyone finally on their feet.

Leaving Penny, Joyce and Gladys to make their own way down when they felt like it, O.L. set off at a brisk pace muttering something about making up for lost tme. Harry, as he'd intended from the beginning, followed close behind her, Bert, Betty and Mavis bringing up the rear. Nearer the summit, Harry drew level with O.L. and then lengthened his stride to get there before her. O.L. gazed in disbelief at the sight of Harry Birch on the top, arms raised in triumph. Was this the man she'd called a wimp? Swallowing her dented pride, she told him how much his new found stamina had impressed her. As the others arrived, Harry found himself showered with cries of surprise and admiration which he acknowledged graciously with a bow as if taking curtain calls after a starring performance.

On the return leg, Harry saw no need for further exertion and walked down with Mavis and Betty at the back of the group. He had proved his point. On the next two training walks, he again deliberately kept a low profile. Striding Edge on Helvellyn was no place to be rushed and the boulder field below Scafell required caution. No point risking a twisted ankle or worse to underline what he had already proved on Skiddaw. Even so, on both occasions, he made sure he was never more than twenty yards behind the leaders. At the summit cairn on Scafell Pike, he was rewarded with a smile from O.L.

'Welcome to the roof of England,' she shrilled. 'Never thought I'd see you here.'

Harry grinned and waited for Bert to arrive.

'What kept you, Bert?' he inquired. 'Thought you'd gone home. Never mind, it's downhill all the way from now on.'

With the group re-united in the farmhouse café at Seathwaite, O.L. felt that congratulations were due all round. She was now sure they would acquit themselves well in Chamonix. Harry had booked the flights from Liverpool and the minibus from Geneva to their hotel. The train to the airport would allow them two hours before take-off. In a week's time, they would be feasting their eyes on snow-capped peaks and glorious sunsets. She herself had almost finished packing and would advise everyone to wear boots instead of packing them: like that, they would save space and make their cases lighter. Sun-cream and sun-glasses should not be forgotten. Above all, they should remember to put any liquids in their hold baggage.

On the drive home, Gladys told Harry how much she now regretted opting out. Along with Penny and Joyce, she had done all three training walks – the shortened versions, it was true – without a single mishap. It was too late, of course, to change her mind but she now felt more confident on rocky terrain and thought she would have managed well enough in Chamonix, at least on the easier walks.

Harry was genuinely sympathetic. He had always liked Gladys, admiring her cheerfulness and stoic indifference whenever she stumbled and fell over. He recalled her fall from the stepping stones in the Forest of Bowland and her sprained ankle on his Mystery Walk. On both occasions, she had made light of her predicament and refused to be fussed over. Gladys, for her part, viewed Harry with indulgence, chiding him when he overstepped the mark in opposition to O.L. but enjoying his histrionic performances and his light-hearted banter with Bert.

She was well aware that Thurston Ramblers needed a fun-loving extrovert like Harry Birch to counterbalance the high-minded seriousness of their president, her long standing friend, Olive. Gladys's rôle as referee or peace-maker, was to prevent things getting out of hand and maintaining harmony within the club. She had been delighted by the recent improvement in relations between Harry and Olive and wondered if it would continue in Chamonix without her restraining influence.

'We'll just have to wait and see, Gladys,' he replied. 'I've shown I can keep up with O.L. if I feel so inclined but that doesn't mean I'll always follow in her footsteps. Actually, I prefer walking at the back with Penny, Mavis and Joyce. If O.L. gets impatient and wants us all to stride along at her pace, someone's got to calm her down. Anyway, I'll keep you posted. I'm taking my i-pod so I'll be able to send you e-mails.'

Gladys thanked him: she would look forward to having news of their exploits.

SOD'S LAW

The journey to Chamonix got off to a bad start. When the train for Liverpool pulled in to the station, neither Harry nor Bert had arrived and O.L. was fuming.

'I might have guessed we'd have problems with those two,' she muttered, 'we'll just have to leave without them. Maybe they'll meet us at the airport.'

It was Mavis who spotted two men rushing onto the platform as the train was leaving.

'There they are,' she cried. 'At least they've got so far. If they take a taxi, they should get to the airport in time. Thank goodness you booked an early train, Olive.'

O.L.'s reply was inaudible, drowned out by speculation about what could have caused Harry and Bert to miss the train.

'Bert wouldn't want to waste money on a taxi to get to the station, you can be sure about that,' said Penny. 'I bet he caught a bus.'

'Which came late or didn't come at all,' suggested Joyce.

'But they both arrived together,' said Mavis. 'My guess is that Harry offered Bert a lift for free in his taxi and the taxi came late, broke down or had an accident.'

'Whatever the reason, a taxi to the airport will cost them a pretty penny,' added Mike. 'Bert won't like that.'

When they arrived at the airport, there was no sign

of Harry and Bert among the smokers having a last puff before going inside. O.L. asked Mike and Joe to wait there while she stalked off, followed by the remaining six, to locate the Geneva check-in. Although it wasn't due to open for 30 minutes, a dozen people had already formed a queue but Harry and Bert were not among them. Bill was sure they would find them at the check-in when it opened but in the meanwhile, suggested going back to collect Mike and Joe and then heading for the coffee shop.

When they got back to the exit, Harry and Bert were just getting out of their taxi. O.L. did not greet them with open arms. Glaring at Harry, she hoped he had a good explanation for their non-appearance at the station. Everyone had been on tenterhooks.

Harry had been rehearsing his explanation all the way in the taxi. With a captive audience hanging on his every word, he now gave full rein to his theatrical bent.

'Ladies and gentlemen, our late arrival at the station can be attributed solely to my good friend Bert .... to his vanity and to his bravery.'

Harry paused, gratified to see the puzzled expressions surrounding him. Having whetted their curiosity, he went on:

'Why vanity, you ask? Because this morning, when the postman delivered the quarterly electricity bill, Bert's wife reminded him that he was due for his quarterly haircut. Bert looked in the mirror: although his bald pate was as hairless and shiny as ever, he had to admit that maybe a short 'back and sides' was a little overdue. But was it worth a fiver? Bert wrestled with this problem for some time until his wife lost patience.

'Go and get yourself smartened up,' she cried, 'you're a scruff!'

And that, my friends, is what caused Bert to visit the barber this morning.'

O.L. had had enough.

'For goodness' sake, get on with it, Mr Birch. What on earth all this has to do with your being late, I can't imagine.'

'You will, Olive, you will: all will be revealed in the fullness of time. We now come to reason number two, Bert's bravery. On arrival at the barber's, he finds himself in a queue behind a spotty-faced youth with shoulder-length hair, an elderly gent needing a shave and a fractious toddler.

Time is of the essence. Bert is well aware that I am due to collect him in my taxi in 40 minutes. He finally emerges, smartened up and fresh as a daisy, with only 5 minutes to spare. He heads briskly for home, smiling in anticipation of his wife's approval.

It was then, ladies and gentlemen, that Sod's Law intervened. A car out of control narrowly misses him, runs into a shop and bursts into flames. The traffic behind, including my taxi, screeches to a halt. Through the flames and smoke, I make out a man trying to wrench open the passenger door which has jammed. He drags out a screaming woman who is frantically pointing to the back seat. Ignoring the risk of the car exploding, he pulls open the back door, extricates a baby and hands it to the mother. That man, ladies and gentlemen, was none other than our good friend Bert.'

With a flamboyant flourish, Harry invited Bert to

step forward as Mavis and Betty led the applause. Bert, who had been rolling his eyes heavenward during Harry's performance, muttered an embarrassed 'thank you' and looked pointedly at his watch. But Harry had more to say.

'You are no doubt wondering what ensued. As soon as I recognise Bert as the author of these heroic deeds, I jump out of my taxi and tell the driver to wait further down the street. A policeman has now appeared. With his help, Bert manages to free the driver. Someone produces a fire extinguisher and puts out the blaze. Only then am I able to prise Bert from the scene and shepherd him into my waiting taxi. He is not, as you can well imagine, a pretty sight: his face and hands are black and his clothes reek of smoke. What's more, he is limping.

When I get him home, his distraught wife rushes upstairs to lay hands on clean clothes while Bert strips off for a shower. His bags are already packed and there is still a faint chance that we might catch the train. Alas, it is not to be. We get within sight of the station when Bert realises he has forgotten to transfer his wallet and passport from his discarded anorak. We have no choice, ladies and gentlemen, but to retrieve them. I trust you will now understand why we failed to catch the train and absolve the noble Bert and myself of blame.'

O.L. had been shuffling from one foot to the other during Harry's speech.

'I think we've all got the picture Mr Birch' she announced. 'I propose we now go back to the check-in. Please keep together. I don't want anyone disappearing into shops, cafés or toilets. Getting lost in a busy airport is all too easy.'

'Not so fast, Olive,' cried Harry, 'Bert has a painful bruise on his shin. Maybe we should ask for one of those electric buggies. What do you think, Bert?'

'Forget it, Harry,' came the quick reply, 'I'll manage.'

When Penny offered to wheel his case, he muttered, none too graciously, 'if you like' and limped along in the wake of O.L. Using her trolley as a battering ram she forced a way through the crowd to arrive at the check-in where a large school party of noisy teenagers in the queue earned her disapproval. She wasn't amused either by Harry's comments on the size of her case.

'Not exactly travelling light, Olive, are we?' he enquired innocently. 'You're not emigrating, are you?'

'No I am not,' she snapped, 'and I doubt if my case weighs much more than yours.'

'Bert's is no light weight either,' added Penny, pointing to the heavily scuffed pigskin holdall she had wheeled to the check-in. 'You must have had that a while, Bert.'

'Family heirloom, that.' interspersed Harry. 'Your dad brought it back from Malaya in the sixties, right Bert? That jungle-green hat you're wearing as well if I'm not mistaken.'

'They'll see me out,' Bert replied.

As long as Harry had known him from their primary school days, Bert had never been at the cutting edge of fashion. As a lad in short pants, he'd worn his elder brother's cast-offs. Money had been tight in those days and food took precedence over clothes. It still did with Bert although, as a plumber never out of work, he could easily afford to splash out on the latest gear that Harry wore. Pressurised by his wife to make himself look halfway decent for his holiday, he had spent all his spare time in the past week trawling round charity shops. For less than a tenner, he'd acquired a yellow and brown checked T-shirt, a dark green fleece and, his pride and joy, a nearly-new bright red anorak with detachable hood and enough pockets to satisfy a conjuror.

The shirt and fleece were now safely in his hold-all but he'd had to abandon the red anorak: blackened and charred, it was ruined beyond repair. It was this, more than his bruised shin, that annoyed Bert. He'd had to resurrect the old anorak which had served him well for fifteen years but now, according to his wife, no self-respecting tramp would give it a second glance. Standing next to Harry, immaculate as ever, made him feel worse. He'd already had enough of Harry's outpourings and was in no mood to hear more. Dropping back in the queue, followed by Penny still wheeling his bag, he sought refuge next to Mike and Joe.

'Looks like you could do with a drink, Bert,' said Mike, producing a flask from his rucksack. 'Fancy a wee dram of Glenfiddich?'

'If you prefer coffee, I've got some here,' added Penny, delving into her bag.

Bert said he'd prefer the whisky to start with but a coffee to follow would be very acceptable. But couldn't Penny herself do with a dram? Given her fear of flying, it might help to steady her nerves. Penny said she'd intended to do just that before boarding but if Mike could spare a drop now, she wouldn't refuse.

As the queue edged forward, O.L. followed the example of the teacher with the school party in making sure everyone in her group had passports and tickets at the ready.

'Thinks we're like kids,' muttered Harry to Mavis.

There were no problems at the check-in but when they got to Security, O.L. was dismayed by the length of the queue snaking round the interminable barriers. Looking anxiously at her watch, she announced that they had only forty five minutes before take-off and would have to forego the coffee Bill had proposed before the arrival of Harry and Bert.

'If anyone's desperate, I've still got some in my flask,' chimed in Penny.

'You've what?' shrieked O.L. 'I told you liquids aren't allowed through Security. Look at that notice over there. There's a bag full of discarded bottles next to it.'

'And that whisky, Mike,' cried Bert, 'it's still in your rucksack, isn't it?'

'Well, you'll have to get rid of it, and the coffee,' snapped O.L. 'Pour them out.'

'Pour them out?' exclaimed Harry, 'Not on your life! We'll drink them here and now! If you need any help, Mike, there'll be no shortage of volunteers. And I'm sure the ladies will see off the coffee.'

O.L.'s spluttered protests were ignored as Mike and Penny passed their flasks round the group whose raised voices and giggles soon began to attract attention. People in front of them were finding the scene quite entertaining, a relief from the boredom of queueing, but those held up behind were clearly not amused. Nor was O.L. who distanced herself from them, leaving Harry to usher the group to one side when it became obvious that they were causing an obstruction.

A further ten minutes meandering round the barriers, brought them almost to the front of the queue when Joyce discovered that she couldn't find her boarding pass. Handing her passport to Penny, she began a frantic search through her handbag and the pockets of her anorak. She was just about to rush back through the queue when Penny found it ... inside the passport Joyce had been clutching ever since leaving the check-in. Everyone, not least the passengers held up behind them in the queue, was relieved but O.L showed no signs of being amused. Striding forward, she deposited her rucksack and anorak in the trays provided and passed under the electronic detector arch only to suffer the indignity of being stopped, searched and told to go back and remove her boots.

'Remove my boots? Ridiculous!' she exclaimed. 'Well, the least you can do is offer me a chair.'

O.L. was politely informed that she would find a chair beyond the barrier where she could take off her boots. Gesturing to the others to do likewise, she put her boots in a tray on the conveyor and again passed under the arch, this time without being stopped. Harry gallantly offered the chair to Joyce while he and the others squatted on the floor to remove their boots. Harry's, which were brand-new and gleaming, drew admiring glances from Mavis and Betty but Bert, who had perked up considerably since helping Mike to finish his whisky, remarked drily that he hoped they wouldn't lose their shine going through the x-ray.

'Well that's one thing you don't have to worry

about,' retorted Harry, 'those boots of yours stopped shining ten years ago. If I were you, I'd fill them with compost and make them into hanging baskets: they'd look well above your front door.'

Bert grinned. There was still plenty of mileage in his boots but when the time came to hang them up, he'd bear in mind Harry's suggestion. In the meantime, he hoped Harry had a good supply of plasters to cope with blisters and chafed ankles in the week ahead.

After passing under the arch without incident, the group retrieved their belongings and were putting their boots back on when Mavis caught sight of O.L., detained by a uniformed official who was inspecting the contents of her rucksack. Mavis rushed forward to hear O.L. protesting indignantly.

'My good man, I object strongly to my time being wasted like this. I can assure you there are no prohibited substances in my rucksack.'

'I'm afraid the x-ray thinks otherwise, madam. This tube, for example.'

'Tube? What tube? Oh, my hand cream. Surely you're not going to tell me that's banned!'

'I'm afraid so, madam. I shall have to put it in the disposal bag you see over there along with all the other tubes, bottles, containers and metallic objects.'

'Just a minute, Olive,' interspersed Mavis, 'you can't allow that! Why not use it up now? I daresay your hands could do with a little pampering right now, mine too.'

'And mine,' added Betty and Joyce who had just arrived.

After a moment's hesitation, O.L. retrieved her

cream and squirted it on three outstretched pairs of hands and then on her own. When their girlish giggles brought Harry and Bert to the scene, O.L., in an unprecedented display of jollity, offered them the rest of the cream.

'Why not?' said Harry, 'I doubt if it'll do much for your leathery paws, Bert, but it's worth a try and it smells nice. Make a change from blocked drains.'

Bert agreed. He'd once told Harry that his annual expenditure on scented soap, after-shave, talcum powder and deodorant amounted to precisely nothing. His wife and sister invariably presented him with such things at Christmas and he made them last all year.

When O.L. had finished plastering cream on the hands of Harry and Bert, she disposed of the empty tube, put on her boots and briskly led the way to the departure lounge.

Looking up at the board, she announced that their flight to Geneva, scheduled to take-off on time in twenty minutes, left from Gate 12.

'Just time for me to nip into the Duty-Free,' said Harry, 'I'll be back in a minute.'

'I'll have to find a loo.' added Joyce, 'I shouldn't have drunk that coffee. Will you come with me Penny?'

'You'll find a loo near the gate, Joyce,' snapped O.L., 'we haven't time to hang about here waiting for you ... or for Mr Birch.'

Boarding had already started when they got to the gate ... without Harry. O.L. could not contain herself.

'He had an excuse for missing the train,' she hissed to Mavis, 'but he's only himself to blame if he misses the plane. The man's totally irresponsible. He's a liabiity.'

It wasn't until they were told that the gate would have to be closed in two minutes that Harry appeared breathless, carrying a large carrier bag.

'Got them,' he gasped to Mavis, 'presents for Monique and her uncle. Couldn't go empty-handed, could we?'

On the plane, Harry found himself sitting next to Syd, a man of few words except on the subject of rugby when he and Bill, his fellow Welshman, would engage in animated discussion incomprehensible to anyone else within earshot. It wasn't long before Syd nodded off, his snoring only partially muffled by the throb of the engine. After indulging in coffee and a sandwich from the trolley, Harry also fell asleep, only waking up when Mavis tapped him on the shoulder and told him they were about to land.

FIRST IMPRESSIONS

O.L. wore a worried frown as they waited to show their passports and went on to reclaim their baggage.

'You've confirmed our time of arrival with the minibus company, I assume?' she asked Harry. 'Did you specify where to meet the driver? How will you recognise him?'

'Fear not, Olive, everything's under control. Our driver has been instructed to station himself at the exit from bagage reclaim holding aloft a board on which will be written the word HARRY. A small prize will be given to whoever spots him first.'

As they emerged dragging their cases, they were confronted by a number of men holding up boards seeking to make contact with Fritz, Jean-Paul, Vladimir, Igor, Madame Leblanc, Senora Bellini, Chi Wan and Czerwinski. Harry's name was nowhere to be seen.

'What now?' asked O.L. grimly, automatically assuming that the non-appearance of the driver was entirely Harry's fault.

'We wait,' said Harry calmly.

'You did give him the right day ... and the right time, I suppose?'

'I did,' Harry replied. 'Now if you'd all be good enough to wait here, I'm going walkabout. Our driver's probably having a smoke outside. Fancy a breath of Swiss air, Bert?'

O.L regretted leaving the arrangements to Harry. If she herself had made them, the driver would have been waiting there half an hour before the plane was due to land, just in case they arrived early.

In the absence of Harry and Bert, Mavis asked everyone to gather round.

'Joyce and I had an idea on the plane,' she began. 'What about all of us clubbing together to buy Bert a new anorak? His wife wasn't joking when she said no self-respecting tramp would give a second look at that scruffy thing he's wearing now. He was really upset at having to bin the red one he'd only just bought.'

Following the nods of agreement all round, Mavis went on:

'I know a very good outdoor shop in Chamonix. We could stop there before going on to the hotel. If everyone contributed 10€, I'm sure we'd find a decent anorak for 100€. Somebody would have to distract Bert's attention while Joyce and I bought it and smuggled it back on to the bus. You could present it to him, Olive, after dinner. What do you think?'

Everybody thought it a good idea and O.L just had time to say she'd be pleased to do the honours when Harry and Bert re-appeared with a fresh-faced young man, obviously the missing driver. After introducing himself as Jean-Michel, he explained, in faultless English, that he'd been held up by heavy traffic in the city centre and apologised for his late arrival.

Walking to the carpark, Mavis found an opportunity to tell Harry about the plan to buy Bert a new anorak. As she had anticipated, Harry was in full agreement: in his opinion, 10€ was a very small price to pay to see the last of Bert's disgusting old anorak. If Mavis needed more than 10€, he would gladly cover the shortfall.

The drive through Geneva was slow but passing through the customs posts into France proved to be a formality and they made up time on the A 40 motorway. Mavis, who had done this journey to Chamonix a year ago when she visited Monique, told them it was called the Route Blanche because in the winter months, the mountains on both sides were covered in snow. At Le Fayet, where the 80 mile stretch of motorway ended, a spectacular viaduct would take them a further 10 miles up to Chamonix. Estimating that the journey would take about 90 minutes, she sent a text message to Monique saying they were on time and were looking forward to meeting her at the hotel.

As they approached Chamonix, she asked the driver to stop in the centre on the pretext that one of the group needed a toilet stop. She didn't want them all, particularly Bert, trooping into the outdoor shop, or any other shop for that matter – she'd never get them out – so asked them to be patient; she and Joyce would be back in five minutes. In the event, it took rather longer. The shop was crowded with bargain hunters drawn by the large red notice in the window proclaiming '*Soldes – Prix Choc!*' By the time they had chosen and bought an anorak the right size, colour and price, it was 15 minutes before they got back to the minibus. to find O.L. in animated conversation with Jean-Michel. Of the others, there was no sign.

'They've just gone to look at postcards in that shop over there,' explained O.L. calmly, 'they'll be back in a minute.'

Mavis and Joyce exchanged glances. O.L. hated being kept waiting and they'd expected to find her champing at the bit. Now, she didn't seem remotely concerned by the absence of the others.

'What a glorious sight!' she enthused, waving her arms all around. 'Jean-Michel's been pointing out some of the landmarks. That's Mont-Blanc up there: you can just see its rounded summit covered with snow. I've already taken a dozen photos.'

Mavis found space in her rucksack for Bert's new anorak before the others returned, Harry bringing up the rear.

'Couldn't resist these,' he told Mavis, showing her a pack of 20 slides of the Chamonix Valley. 'They're an insurance policy. If my own don't turn out too well, I'll show these at the camera club. They're brilliant, don't you think?'

'I'll look at them in the bus,' Mavis replied curtly, rather niggled that he'd forgotten to ask about Bert's anorak. 'It's time we were moving. Monique will be wondering where we've got to.'

It took another 10 minutes to arrive at the village of Les Praz and locate the hotel, a three storey building largely covered by Virginia Creeper with boxes of red geraniums at every window. When the cases had been unloaded, Harry called for a group photo and asked Jean-Michel if he would oblige. Just then Monique came running up to greet them all with kisses on both cheeks. Syd, who only showed emotion at rugby matches, reacted rather sheepishly to her embrace but Harry and Bert were much more enthusiastic.

'Welcome to beautiful Chamonix,' cried Monique, 'I 'ope – oops, sorry Harry – I hope you had a pleasant journey. You must come and meet my uncle Claude. Then I will show you your rooms. We will eat at 8 o'clock in the garden on this warm, sunny evening. I think it is maybe too late for tea, is it not?'

'It's never too late for tea, Monique.' replied Bert.

'Forget your tea for once, Bert,' interposed Harry. 'It's past 6. I'll treat you, and anyone else who's interested, to a beer instead... after our patient friend here, Jean-Michel, has taken a photo of our arrival. I'd like you in the middle, Monique, flanked by Olive and Mavis. And Bert, if you wouldn't mind removing your anorak.'

Uncle Claude restricted himself to hand-shakes all round, which was a relief to Syd. O.L., introduced by Monique as '*Madame la Présidente*,' was also favoured with a bow. Claude hoped that the group would very much enjoy their stay; if they encountered any problems, they should not hesitate to inform him About food, for example, did anyone have any allergies?

Harry got in before O.L., who had no patience with what she termed 'fussy eaters,' to say that Penny was a vegetarian; she had no problem with eggs but she didn't eat meat or fish. A faint expression of disbelief crept over the hotelier's face, accompanied by a Gallic shrug. No matter, he would make sure that madame was offered alternative dishes. As for tonight's meal, he assumed everyone would enjoy the cheese dish, *fondue sayoyarde*, a speciality of the region. O.L. promptly proclaimed that they would all be very happy to partake of this dish – and of any other regional specialities he cared to set before them.

While the others were shown to their rooms by Monique, Mavis and Betty joined Harry and Bert in the bar. Bert was not impressed by the draught beer.

'Supped worse,' was his blunt verdict, 'but not often.'

A second glass, this time a Belgian beer recommended by Mavis, was more to his liking but he was alarmed by the price and glad he wasn't footing the bill. When Monique reappeared, she announced that the three single rooms for O.L., Syd and Harry were on the top floor.

'Need any help with your luggage, Harry?' Bert asked, poker-faced.

'Very kind of you to offer, old pal, particularly in view of your gammy leg, but no thanks. I'm just relieved it's me up there, not you. I'd have felt obliged to carry you as well as your luggage.'

Bert was still wearing his old anorak when he joined the others for the evening meal in the garden. In sharp contrast, Harry was resplendent in beige trousers, dark blue Aran sweater, yellow shirt and brown suede shoes. The ladies, without exception, wore long skirts and either frilly blouses or colourful tops along with ear-rings, necklaces, bangles, broaches, eye-shade, face powder, lipstick and in the case of Penny and Joyce, painted fingernails.

'Don't think we've met,' said Bert to Joyce, 'Do you come here often?'

'My mother taught me never to speak to strange men,' retorted Joyce, moving away from him to sit next to Penny.

The sunset cast a rosy glow over the long trestle table covered with blue and white checked cloths and adorned with vases of flowers and an array of red, white and blue candles which would be lit later when the sun had gone in. After chicken soup to start, three casseroles of melted cheese, each to be shared by four people, were placed on lighted burners. Alongside each was a basket containing small cubes of bread. Mavis explained.

'The idea is to spear the bread with your two-pronged fork and twirl it round in the cheese. When it's nicely coated, lift it out, give it another twirl to avoid drips, wait a few seconds to let it cool and then eat it. Easy. Like this.'

'But you must not let your bread fall into the cheese, *n'est-ce pas?*' cried Monique. 'If you do, you must pay *un gage*! *C'est quoi, en anglais,* Mavis?'

'Oh yes, you have to pay a forfeit. You needn't look so worried, Syd. It's just for a laugh. By the way, you should lower the flame when the cheese thickens. And help yourselves to the wine: it's a dry white, very good with *fondue* – helps digest the cheese.'

Harry was the first to follow Mavis's instructions. Watched closely by the others, he attached the bread to his fork, immersed it into the bubbling cheese and gave it a twirl. With a cry of *voilà,* he lifted it high in the air and continued to twirl, basking in the applause from all around. Harry's moment of triumph was short-lived: he gave his fork one twirl too many and the bread, too thickly coated with cheese, slid back down into the pan.

'Forfeit, forfeit, forfeit,' chanted eleven voices in unison.

Bert suggested he be made to drink nothing but water for the rest of the evening. Joyce thought a strip-tease act would be fun but O.L. said that would be letting him off too lightly. What if he were to do twenty press-ups on the lawn? It was finally left to Monique to decide on a suitable forfeit. She would like to hear Harry singing a song, an English folksong. Bert said that would be more of a punishment for **them** but Harry, had jumped to his feet, only too willing to oblige.

'Ladies and gentlemen, it gives me great pleasure to entertain you with that much loved Yorkshire dialect song 'Ilkla Moor b'aht 'at.' For the benefit of Monique – and for Syd and Bill who had the misfortune to be born in Wales, the song gives a dire warning to a young man who goes courting on Ilkley Moor without wearing a hat. He will catch his death of cold. When he is buried, he will be eaten by worms. The worms will then be eaten by ducks and the ducks will end up being eaten by his friends – who will, in due course, be eating him! Please feel free to join in the chorus.'

Pointing an accusing finger at Bert, Harry let rip.
Where hast tha been since I saw thee?
On Ilkla Moor b'aht 'at
Where hast tha been since I saw thee?
Where hast tha been since I saw thee?
Altogether now everyone.
On Ilkla Moor b'aht 'at
On Ilkla Moor b'aht 'at.

Once Harry had started, there was no stopping him. Before all the verses had been sung, diners at other tables dotted around the garden were joining in the chorus. Even O.L., not normally appreciative of Harry's performances, ended up singing with gusto, helped by the wine to which she'd obviously taken a liking.

Harry was not the only one to let his bread fall into the cheese. Joyce protested that Bert had nudged her arm at a critical moment but her cries went unheard. Vowing to have her revenge on Bert, she too agreed to sing a song. Hand on heart, she gave a soulful rendering of 'She's a lassie from Lancashire,' the last two lines bringing rapturous applause.

None could be fairer or rarer than Sarah,

My lassie from Lancashire.

During a lull in the conversation, O.L. surprised everyone by suggesting having a fondue at the club's Christmas dinner. Harry was immediately enthusiastic.

'Splendid idea, Olive. I'm sure my good friend at the Ploughman's Arms will oblige. Will you give us the recipe, Monique?'

'With pleasure, Arry. It is very easy to make. We use Beaufort and Emmental cheese but I suppose any hard cheese will be O.K. You will need garlic, Kirsch liqueur and of course, dry white wine. I will write it all down for you.'

'*Tu es très gentille,*' replied Harry, sporting his recently acquired French, '*Merci bien.*'

When the cheese had thickened beyond redemption, the casseroles were whisked away and replaced by individual *tartes aux myrtilles* liberally topped with fresh cream. Bert offered to help out Penny if she was dieting but his generous offer was curtly refused. As coffee was being served, Mavis slipped away to return with a bulky carrier bag. It was time to present Bert with his new anorak.

Rather unsteadily, O.L. rose to her feet, called for attention and began her speech. Bert had rolled his eyes heavenwards at the airport when Harry gave his account of events but now O.L.'s lurid version made him squirm with embarrassment. When she at last produced the anorak and called him forward to try it on, Harry cried 'speech, speech.'

'Nay, Harry, we've had enough speeches for one day,' he blurted out, 'but thank you all very much. Very good of you, I'm sure.'

'What are you going to do with the old one, Bert?' asked Mavis.

Harry gave him no time to answer.

'The least we can do is give it a good send-off. Give it the last rites before we cremate it. You could take the ashes home in a jar, Bert, as a present to your wife.'

Monique found Harry's proposal very droll. Uncle Claude had an incinerator he used for burning rubbish; she would go and find it at once ... and a can of petrol.

With all the group standing solemnly round, Harry dropped a match on Bert's anorak declaring 'Sic transit gloria Berti' as flames rose in the air. Bert looked doleful. When he didn't join in the general applause, Harry put an arm round his shoulder and sought to console him.

'Cheer up, old pal, You must admit you've had your money's worth out of it.'

'Ay, that's true: served me well, did that anorak,' muttered Bert. 'They were made to last in those days.'

Monique wished them all pleasant dreams before driving back home to Chamonix: she would return after breakfast for their first walk.

It was some time before Mavis and Betty fell asleep. So much had happened since they left home that morning. So many things to talk about.

'Brilliant idea of yours to get Bert a new anorak,' Joyce began. 'You'd think he'd won the lottery when he tried it on and gave those twirls. Fits like a glove. Never seen him look so smart. His wife will be pleased she's seen the last of his old one.'

'Won't we all,' exclaimed Mavis, 'especially Harry. He was in his element tonight. Really enjoyed singing 'Ilkla Moor b'aht 'at' and getting everyone to join in.'

'Wouldn't be surprised if it wasn't deliberate, dropping his bread into the cheese. He never misses the chance of an audience, does he. He even got O.L. going!'

'I think the wine had something to do with that,' replied Mavis. 'Did you notice her speech was a bit blurred? Anyway, she certainly let her hair down. Never seen her so relaxed.'

'Let's hope she stays that way for the whole week,' added Joyce, 'though I wouldn't bet on it. Harry's bound to say something or do something to upset her.'

LE CHALET DU CHAPEAU

Harry's didn't complain about his room on the top floor. Quite the reverse. The walk-in shower and separate W.C. came as no surprise but what he had not expected was a balcony looking out on the snow-capped peaks of the Mont-Blanc range. A view to die for.

After last night's jollifications, he had not bothered to close the shutters before sinking into bed and it was the sun streaming through the window that woke him up at 7 a.m. Camera in hand, he went on to the balcony to take what would surely be a prize-winning photo in his camera club's annual exhibition. After several shots of the stunning mountain scenery, he was just about to take photos of the village when he noticed in the street below the unmistakeable figure of O.L., camera in one hand and map in the other. Harry thought of giving her a shout, asking if she'd slept well after all the wine she'd drunk but decided against it. He'd probably disturb the others, still no doubt in the land of Nod.

O.L. was dismayed to find herself alone in the dining room for breakfast at the appointed time of 8 a.m. She knew it was self-service but all the same, she couldn't repress a frown as the others arrived in dribs and drabs. Last in was Bert at 8.30, wearing his new anorak and beaming like the cat that got the cream. Harry led the applause and Bert responded with twirls and bows to all the ladies.

'There's fruit juice over there,' Mavis told him, 'and you help yourself to coffee, chocolate or hot water.'

'Where's the teapot?' asked Bert.

'You'll be lucky!' replied Harry. 'Fill your cup with hot water and choose a tea bag: you can have Indian, Chinese, Sri Lankan, Earl Grey or herbal.'

Bert didn't fancy any of those: he only drank Co-op tea. In the end he settled for milky coffee which he obviously found drinkable as he went back four times for refills.

In the absence of porridge and Shredded Wheat, one of which always preceded his breakfast fry-up at home, he filled a bowl with corn flakes and added two spoonfuls of apple puree and one of stewed apricots. A warm croissant was followed by two bread rolls, the first converted into a cheese and ham butty, the second smothered with strawberry jam.

'Are you quite sure you've had enough, Bert?' asked Joyce.

'It'll keep me going till lunch time,' replied Bert, 'but just to make sure, I'll have a slice of that rice cake and a banana.'

Monique appeared as arranged at 9 o'clock. In yellow shorts, pale blue sleeveless top, dark brown bandana and all over tan, she could have stepped straight out of a health and fitness magazine. Harry insisted on a photo as she spread the map on a table in the garden and began to talk about the day's walk.

'Our first walk is not 'ard, you will be pleased to know, 'Arry. It is a *mise en jambes*. 'Ow you say that in English, Mavis?'

When Mavis said it was like a warm-up before the serious walking began, Monique went on to say it would only take about four hours, not counting stops. They would take the path through a forest of spruce and larch to a viewpoint overlooking the *Gorges de l'Aveyron*. Then there was a steady climb up to the *Chalet du Chapeau* at 1576 metres where they would see the *moraine* below the glacier, called *la Mer de Glace.*

Penny and Joyce exchanged worried looks at Monique's casual mention of 1576 metres but Mavis pointed out that as they were already at 1060 metres, they would only have 516 metres to climb. It was just a little bit higher than Pen-y-Ghent, after all.

'You'll be roasting in that anorak, Bert,' said Harry, 'best leave it behind. It isn't going to rain today, you'll be sorry to hear. The forecast promises sun all day.'

Seeing the amount of exposed white flesh all around, Monique advised everyone to apply sun cream before they set off and to make sure they had enough water – at least a litre each. Lip salve might also be a good idea for the ladies.

'And for Bert.' added Harry.

'I'll use some of yours,' retorted Bert, 'and the mascara, if you've any left.'

Neither Penny nor Joyce had remembered to pack sun cream and they all, with one exception, needed more water. No problem, said Monique, they could get everything they needed at the mini-market where they were going to buy their picnics. O.L. was not pleased to hear this. She had already applied sun cream, filled her water bottle from the tap and with enough cheese sandwiches and an apple left over from the journey, she didn't need a picnic.

'I hope we won't be wasting time like this every morning,' she exclaimed. 'I suggest we buy enough food now to last three or four days – or buy picnics the night before.'

After half an hour in the shop, even Harry conceded O.L. had a point. Monique's help was in great demand: dashing here and there, she recommended this, advised against that, pointing out what was good value and what was expensive. Bert slowed things down even more by wanting every price converted from euros into pounds. In the end, when he kept muttering rip-off, Harry told him to let the moths out of his purse. With all the money he saved on hair cream and his quarterly visits to the barber, he could afford to eat like a king.

Outside the shop, O.L. paced up and down like a caged lion. When all the group had finally emerged, carrier bags in hand, it was clear they'd have to return to the hotel to deposit what wasn't needed for the day's walk. This further delay did nothing to improve O.L.'s mood. Seeing her striding out ahead, Monique called out:

'We 'ave plenty of time, Olive. There is really no need to 'urry.'

'I must say your English has improved, Monique, since last year,' commented Harry as they walked back to the hotel, 'even if you still have trouble with your aitches. Come to that, so does Bert, so who cares?'

'*Merci monsieur*,' replied Monique, '*Et vous?* Mavis has told me you have been taking French lessons. Can you say *le vin blanc qu'on a bu hier avec la fondue était très bon?*'

'Too early in the day,' answered Harry, 'my vocal cords would need a lot of lubricating before I could manage all that. Maybe this evening, after a glass or two.'

Back at the hotel, O.L. and Monique found a seat in the garden while the others went up to their rooms to leave behind their surplus food.

'It's a lovely view of the mountains, is it not?' said Monique in an attempt to defuse O.L.'s impatience. 'I am so pleased the weather is perfect for our first walk.'

'If we ever get started,' replied O.L. darkly, looking at her watch. 'We've been here five minutes. What on earth's keeping them?'

There were several explanations for what was keeping them. Chief among them was the joint decision of Mavis, Betty, Penny and Joyce to follow the example of Monique and change into shorts. Harry and Syd, after climbing to the top floor, had forgotten to collect their room keys from reception while Bert and Bill had looked in vain for their key on the board until Bert remembered he'd put it in his pocket. But which pocket? Mike and Joe, as organised as O.L. herself, were the first to emerge and the only ones to escape O.L.'s baleful looks.

'Glad to see you've brought your stick, Bert,' called Harry as they finally set off, 'you'll need all the help you can get with that gammy leg.'

'Just a precaution,' replied Bert, 'The arnica Monique rubbed on it last night seems to have cured it. Don't think I'll be needing Mountain Rescue.'

Monique pricked up her ears at the mention of Mountain Rescue. They would soon be passing the *héliport* where helicopters took off to rescue climbers and walkers in distress.

Her brother, Henri, was actually based there as a *secouriste* in the *Peloton de Gendarmerie de Haute Montagne*. He had told her many fascinating stories of rescues in the mountains. Mike, ex-police sergeant and one time member of a mountain rescue team in the Lake District, was particularly interested in everything Monique could tell them. When they reached the base, a helicopter was just about to land and Monique had to wait for the noise to subside to make herself heard.

'It is a very dangerous job, you know. They rescue skiers who have fallen into crevasses, walkers who have been swept away by avalanches and climbers who have become stranded on ledges high up in the mountains. They save many lives but there are days they can't take off because of blizzards or strong winds and then it is often too late to find any survivors. Sometimes Henri says they can't even locate the bodies.'

'Makes my blood run cold just to think about it,' cried Penny.

'But my brother enjoys his job: he wanted to be a *secouriste* ever since he was a small boy. He trained for one year to be a *gendarme* and then another year to become a rescuer. He has to keep himself very fit so he goes skiing and running in the mountains. He is never bored: there are so many calls for help all the year round. It is not surprising really because in the Chamonix Valley we have about 25,000 visitors in winter and 100,000 in summer, most of them skiers, climbers and walkers.'

Mike said he could see why a professional rescue

service was needed. In the Lake District, mountain rescue teams were almost all unpaid volunteers, local men and women who depended on fund-raising events and legacies to meet the cost of administration, buying and maintaining vehicles, acquiring equipment and training rescue dogs. People they brought down to safety were not obliged to pay for their rescue although most made a donation.

Monique was surprised to learn this. Mountain rescue was very costly, especially when helicopters were needed and skiers, climbers and walkers in France were expected to take out insurance to cover it. As well as medical treatment and repatriation.

'And so they should!' exclaimed Harry. 'It's the least they can do. People who go skiing or climbing mountains have no right to expect free rescue if they get into trouble.'

'You have a point, Harry,' interrupted Mike, 'but you know rescuers in the U.K. see it differently. We prefer to keep it free. If mountain rescue were charged for, people would have to take out insurance. Can you imagine every walker climbing Pen-y-Ghent or Cat Bells being insured against mountain rescue? It just wouldn't happen. Of course, you can't compare the Lake District to the Chamonix Valley. When I was in the Langdale/Ambleside team, we had about a hundred calls for help a year; here in Chamonix, they probably have ten times as many, way beyond the scope of part-time volunteers. And the cost of running a fully professional rescue service must be horrendous. No wonder they expect you to be insured.'

'I hope we are, Olive,' cried Joyce, 'You don't have to be a skier or a mountaineer to have an accident. It can happen to anyone. Remember what happened to me last year on Scafell; a little slip was all it took to knock me out.'

'It's something I'm not likely to forget, Joyce. We had to abort our walk to Scafell Pike because of it. I hope you'll be extra careful this week ... and yes, we are insured. Now can we get moving, Monique, we've hardly walked a mile so far.'

Further discussion about mountain rescue was suspended as they walked in single file through a forest of spruce and larch up to the viewpoint looking down on the source of the river Arveyron emerging from the terminal moraine of the *Mer de Glace*. On the other side of the gorge, the spectacular red *Rochers des Mottets* towered 400 metres above them. Squeals of delight came from Penny and Joyce. They had only climbed 200 metres and this was their first close-up view of alpine scenery. O.L. too was clearly impressed but as soon as her photos had been taken, she wanted to press on.

'Hold your horses, Olive,' called out Harry, 'we haven't a bus to catch. It's time for elevenses anyway and Bert looks like he could do with a drink'

Monique thought they should all have a drink. It was important to drink little and often in the mountains to avoid dehydration even if one didn't feel thirsty. Besides, they had 300 metres climbing ahead of them to get to the *Chalet du Chapeau* and in this sun, they would certainly be perspiring.

In the shade of the forest, the sun wasn't a problem but when they emerged and joined an exposed, rocky uphill track, the heat began to take its toll. Penny, Joyce and Betty were flagging and Joe dropped behind to give them moral support. What struck him at once was the redness of their legs. Apparently, none of them had thought of putting sun cream on their legs when they changed from trousers into shorts. Unprotected legs could lead to sunstroke, he told them, just as easily as unprotected arms, shoulders, neck and face. They must stop and cream up straight away.

Joe called the others back but O.L. had the wind in her sails and was too far ahead to hear him. Harry told Monique not to worry; it was high time that O.L. learned to walk behind the leader, not in front. When she realised nobody was following her, she'd be back.

Bert's offer to help Joyce apply cream to her legs was met by a curt rejection.

'Never mind about my legs, Bert, put an extra thick layer on your bald pate. That floppy hat you've acquired won't keep the sun out. Still, it's an improvement on that scruffy old bobble hat you wore on Scafell: you looked like Compo in Last of the Summer Wine.'

Like Joe, Mike recognised the importance of adequate protection against the sun. 'It's a bit like shutting the stable door after the horse has bolted,' he commented. 'but I think you'll be O.K. If you can't sleep tonight, try calamine lotion or something similar.'

'What does Mike mean about an 'orse. Mavis?' asked Monique.''Ow can an 'orse bolt a door? It is a joke, is it not?'

Mavis explained that when a horse bolted, it ran away. It was no good shutting the stable door after the horse had run away. Monique pondered this a moment before exclaiming triumphantly:

'Now I understand. We 'ave a saying like that, *prendre des précautions après coup.* I 'ope it is not too late to prevent them getting sunburnt. But I think *mieux vaut tard que jamais.* Do you know that one, 'Arry?'

'Can't say it springs readily to mind, Monique, but at a guess I suppose we'd say better late than never. Like when Bert goes to have his hair cut every four months.' Bert made a rude gesture but had no time to retaliate as O.L. was seen striding towards them looking anything but pleased and Harry was striding out to greet her, arms outstretched.

'Madam Johnstone, I presume,' he exclaimed.

O.L. was not amused. Brushing aside his offer of an emotional reunion, she demanded to know the reason for the delay.

'They forgot to cream their legs? I can't believe it! After what Monique told them?'

'Now then Olive, let's not get too upset. There are worse things to forget … like forgetting you're not the leader and forging ahead regardless. Monique was quite worried about you.'

'No need to be,' growled O.L. 'I'm perfectly capable of looking after myself. Now if they've all finished, maybe we can make up for yet more lost time.'

With O.L. following close behind, Monique slowed her pace to avoid demoralising the tail-enders. As the path wound its way up to the chalet, criss-crossing rushing streams, the mountain scenery became more and more photogenic. Harry wanted to stop for photos but Monique advised him to wait until they reached the chalet and the viewpoint over the moraine.

Bert, more concerned with refreshment than photos, gave a whoop of delight when the chalet came into sight. Tables with parasols were set out on a terrace shaded by larch trees and a menu board showed the words *boissons* and *plats*. Bert perused the drinks on offer until he found what he was looking for.

'Fancy a beer, Harry?' he shouted, 'they haven't got Guinness but it's got to be better than tap water.'

'Don't mind if I do, Bert, make it a pint will you? I'll get the coffee later.'

Red faced and dripping with sweat, Penny eased her rucksack off and sank onto the nearest chair, soon to be joined by Joyce, her face wreathed in smiles.

'What a glorious setting!,' she exclaimed. 'the chalet with its red shutters and the window boxes full of flowers … and the sunlight filtering through the trees.'

Penny said she couldn't agree more and what a pity Gladys wasn't with them; she would have been thrilled. They must send her a card showing a photo of the chalet.

Monique had intended going straight on to the glacier viewpoint before returning to picnic at the chalet but no-one showed the slightest inclination to move. Joining Harry and Bert who had already begun to eat, she wished them *bon appétit* and asked how they were enjoying their first day in the mountains.

'*Magnifique,*' cried Harry, waving his arms all round in a theatrical gesture and knocking Bert's hat off in the process. '*N'est-ce pas,* Bert?'

Bert retrieved his hat, nodded and continued to munch his way through the 8 inch long ham and salad *baguette* he'd finally bought on the recommendation of Mavis.

Harry went on to enthuse about the scale and variety of the views all around. They could see Chamonix down below in the valley backed by the stunning *Aiguilles Rouges* while ahead of them, on the Mont-Blanc side of the valley, the jagged skyline had become more and more impressive as they gained height. It was a photographer's dream.

O.L. was of the same opinion. First to finish her picnic, she disappeared, camera in hand, to find the best vantage points. Mike had spread out his 1/25,000 map on a table and he and Joe were reminiscing about walks and climbs they had done some years ago. Joyce went to order a coffee and emerged with a plate of home-made *tarte aux framboises* swimming in cream which she tried unsuccessfully to hide from Bert.

'Forgotten you were on a diet, Joyce?' he called. 'You've enough calories there to last all week. You'll have some explaining to do at Weight-Watchers, I can see that.'

'You could do with a slice of this yourself to put some flesh on your bones,' retorted Joyce. 'But there again, good food is wasted on you: you've nothing to show for it.'

Bert grinned, reminded Harry of his promise to buy the coffee and strolled over to join Bill and Syd who were going to have a look inside the chalet. Round the walls they found old photos of grim-looking mountaineers and guides. A pair of primitive skis hung above the fire-place alongside an equally primitive pair of snowshoes and fixed to the ceiling were ice-axes, crampons and ropes, all of which had seen service in days long gone by.

'With gear like that, no wonder those guys look

grim,' remarked Syd as they came out to find O.L. rucksack on back, looking at her watch and Harry tucking into a *tarte aux framboises* swimming in cream which he'd bought on impulse along with coffee for Bert and himself. It took another five minutes for them to finish eating and drinking and for Joyce to locate the toilet before they were ready to walk the ten minutes to the viewing platform overlooking the moraine of the *Mer de Glace*.

At first, Harry was disappointed. In the V-shaped valley far below, all he could see were two small, milky green, glacial lakes and a mass of stones and rocks. Higher up, where the valley narrowed, were huge, grey blocks with a few white patches of snow here and there. No sign of the towering seracs, ice falls and crevasses he had imagined seeing at close quarters. Aware of his disappointment, Monique explained that the glacier had receded since the middle of the 19th century. Then it came right down to the valley floor at 1000 metres. Now it had retreated to 1500 metres. As it shrunk, rocks trapped in the ice were released and the terminal moraine became longer. The only ice visible was in the huge grey blocks high above the moraine: they would see it better through binoculars.

Harry got out his binoculars but remained unimpressed. The moraine was like a lunar landscape and the dirty grey blocks above showed very few traces of ice. He was impressed however, very much impressed, by the spectacular mountains on both sides of the glacier and the snow covered skyline in the background. Before taking photos, he asked Monique to show him the place names on the map and set the scene.

'The mountain on the left is *Les Drus,* 3754 metres: you can't see the top from here but there is a lovely view of it from *Les Praz,* especially at sunset. On the right, are some of the Chamonix Needles: *l'Aiguille des Grands Charmoz, l'Aiguille du Grépon* and *l'Aiguille de Blaitière.* They are about 3500 metres. On the horizon, we can see *les Grandes Jorasses* covered in snow with *la Dent du Géant,* just over 4,000 metres, in the middle. It will make a wonderful photograph, will it not?'

Harry wasn't the only one to think it would. No-one had a camera as sophisticated as his but they all, without exception, followed his lead and took photos.

O.L in particular was entranced. She had admired photos of the Alps in books and magazines but seeing them at first hand took her breath away. What really attracted her was not so much the beauty of mountains as the challenge they represented. In her eyes, mountains existed to be climbed – that was their *raison d'être* – and climbing them demanded the qualities she most admired, courage, discipline and persevrance of the highest order. Her hero and rôle model, Mr Wainwright, had qualities like these but he always described fell-walkers as 'lesser mortals' compared to mountaineers. Had she been younger, she would have liked nothing better than to pit herself against these giants. They made Snowdon and Scafell Pike look like molehills. She regretted giving up on Mont-Blanc but she knew in her heart of hearts it would have been unwise. At her age, just being in the mountains rather than on top of them was cause enough for satisfaction. It was a pleasure denied to most of her contemporaries, including her friend Gladys. As the group was leaving the viewing platform to go down, she begged leave to say a few words..

'Ladies and gentlemen,' she began, 'I'm sure you would all like me to express our thanks to Monique for inviting us to visit this wonderful area. For most of us, today's walk introducing us to these magnificent mountains, has been a revelation and I've no doubt that the walks to come will be equally, or even more, exhilarating. I personally feel privileged to be here as I'm sure we all do. *Merci beaucoup* Monique.'

'Hear, hear,' cried Harry, leading the applause. 'Couldn't have said it better myself.'

In reply, Monique said she was so pleased they had accepted her invitation and she was delighted to have such an appreciative audience. She had very good memories of her walk with Thurston Ramblers in Teesdale: they were so gay and amusing. She still laughed when she remembered Harry trying to rescue the sheep caught in the wire fence.

'No laughing matter that, Monique,' exclaimed Harry, 'The only thanks I got from that sheep was a kick on the leg!'

'It didn't do your baseball cap any good either,' chipped in Bert.'I can see that sheep now thrashing about in a juniper bush, blindfolded by your cap. You presented it to Monique as a souvenir. Have you still got it Monique?'

'Of course I've still got it!' came the reply. 'I put it on my bedroom wall with the photos Harry sent me of that lovely day.'

O.L. put a stop to further reminiscing by asking if they were taking the same path down. Not exactly, said

Monique, they would join the *Grand Balcon Nord* and then make their way to the hamlet of *Les Bois* missing out the *Gorges de l'Arveyron*. But before they set off, she wanted to say something about tomorrow's walk.

'Today,' she began, 'we have been at the bottom of *La Mer de Glace* : tomorrow, we shall be above it – nearly 300 metres above it! Then we shall go down to it and visit the ice grotto. That will make you very 'appy 'Arry, will it not? Tomorrow, you will see plenty of ice. Inside the glacier, you will be surrounded by ice!'

Harry beamed. Joyce asked if sweaters would be needed and Penny hoped they would not be walking all that way up from the hotel. Monique replied yes to Joyce and no to Penny.

There was a train from Les Praz at 09.03 for the short ride into Chamonix where she would meet them. They would then walk to the *Aiguille du Midi* station and take the cable-car up to the starting point of their walk, *le Plan de l'Aiguille* at 2310 metres.The fare was 12.50 euros.

When Bert pulled a face at this, Mavis wondered if he might prefer to walk up. It would only take about four hours. If he set off at 6 o'clock, he'd get there by 10. As Bert didn't seem much attracted by this option, Harry offered to lend him his stick, if that would help. With two sticks instead of one, he might allow himself another10 minutes in bed. Monique did not understand Bert's rather uncouth reply.

'From the *Plan de l'Aiguille*,' she went on, 'we have a splendid balcony walk looking down over Chamonix and across the valley to the *Aiguilles Rouges*. Then there is a zig-zag climb up to *le Signal Forbes* from where we look down on *la Mer de Glace* and have magnificent views of *les Drus, la Verte et les Grandes Jorasses*.'

'Sounds great, Monique,' interrupted Harry, 'but you haven't mentioned the possibility of liquid refreshment. Mustn't risk getting dehydrated, you know.'

'You mean like today at the *Chalet du Chapeau*? Do not worry, 'Arry, you can get your beer at *Montenvers* when we go down to the glacier. And if you are still thirsty, at the *Chalet de Caillet* on the way back to Les Praz. Now I think we should start going down.'

O.L. needed no encouragement. Forgetting what she'd been told about keeping behind the leader, she strode briskly ahead and was soon out of sight on the winding path.

'Olive is always in a hurry, is she not,' said Monique to Mavis. 'She is not *décontractée* like 'Arry. You told me in Teesdale she thought he was a wimp because he was not a serious walker and he didn't like climbing hills. And he thought she was a dragon.'

'Olive is certainly not as relaxed as Harry,' laughed Mavis, 'but then who is? But both of them have changed since last year. And all thanks to you!'

'Thanks to me? It is not possible! How can that be possible?'

'Well at first, Harry had no desire to come with us to Chamonix; sweating up mountains didn't appeal to him at all. I tried to change his mind by talking about the easy walks on the *Petits Balcons,* the cable-cars and the brilliant photos he could take. But it was only when I quoted from your letter to me that he finally decided to come with us. You said you were very much looking forward to seeing Harry again.'

'So if I had not said that, he would not be here! But you said he had changed. Did you mean in appearance? I knew at once he had lost weight.'

Mavis explained briefly. Having decided to join them in Chamonix, Harry had embarked on a fitness campaign – jogging, exercises and dieting. Everyone, especially Olive, had been amazed at the transformation. Instead of trailing behind, he had been among the first to get up hills, like today for example.'

'So Olive can no longer consider him a wimp!' exclaimed Monique.

'Exactly. Nor can his pal Bert or anyone else. O.L. still thinks he's frivolous and doesn't approve of his jokes or his speechifying but now she respects him as a walker.'

'And does Harry still think she is a dragon?'

'I don't think so. Her new-found respect for him has been mutual. He still thinks she's domineering and humourless but now I think he secretly admires her spirit. They will never be soul-mates but they're more tolerant of each other than they were last year.'

O.L. was waiting for them at the junction, wisely allowing Monique to take the lead.

As they neared the hotel, a helicopter about to land prompted Monique to ask Mike and Joe if they would like to visit the heliport. She was sure her brother would show them round and tell them about his work in mountain rescue. Would they like to do that on the free day if she could arrange it?

'That would be great,' said Mike. 'The others are

probably going up to the *Aiguille du Midi* but we did that when we came last time and were wondering what else to do.'

What Bert was wondering was how to survive the three hour wait for dinner at 8 o'clock. At home, he usually had his evening meal about 6 and that was after a fry-up for breakfast and a decent lunch. Today, all he'd eaten since breakfast was a ham salad baguette a slice of rice cake and a banana. He got no sympathy from Joyce.

'If you hadn't been so tight-fisted, you could have bought a *quiche lorraine* this morning like I did. It was delicious. And so was that raspberry tart and cream at the chalet.'

'Why don't you have a nap, Bert, if you are very hungry,' suggested Monique mischievously. 'We have a saying *qui dort, dîne*. 'Ow you say that in English, Mavis?'

Mavis told Bert that he wouldn't feel hungry if he had a sleep. When Bert snorted at this idea, Harry came up with another one.

'How about a game of *boules*? That would take your mind off food, Bert. There's a *piste* at the bottom of the garden and I've seen a bucket full of *boules*. Suppose we met in an hour after we've had a shower and got changed? Ladies versus gents, how about that?'

Without appearing too regretful, O.L. said she had arranged to explore the neighbourhood with Mike and Joe before dinner but Monique clapped her hands enthusiastically and offered to act as umpire to ensure fair play. Mavis and Betty could play Harry and Bert while Penny and Joyce could play Syd and Bill. Then the winners of each leg could play each other. She would provide prizes for them.

With the exception of Mavis, the nearest any of them had got to French *boules* was seeing children playing with brightly coloured plastic balls in the park or on the beach.

'It's easy,' Mavis explained when all were assembled. 'The *boule* nearest the *cochonnet* or jack scores a point just like in our game of bowls.'

'It seems to me that that's the only thing they have in common,' said Bill, looking at the rough gravelly *piste.* The groundsman at my bowling club would have a fit at the very thought of playing on a surface like that.'

'But that's the beauty of *boules*,' replied Mavis. 'You don't need a manicured green, you can play just about anywhere. It's very informal. When they play matches, you won't see teams dressed in white, wearing flat shoes in case they damage the green.'

Bert was examining two *boules* he'd picked at random from the bucket.

'Your groundsman would have another fit, Bill, if bowls like these were raining down on his green. They're like cannon balls; they must weigh nearly two pounds.'

It took several minutes for everyone to find matching pairs of *boules,* identified by the patterns engraved on their surface, before play could begin. As the *piste* was not big enough for both matches to take place simultaneously, Bill, Syd, Penny and Joyce offered to let the others play first and demonstrate their skill.

Mavis won the toss. Standing inside the circle she had drawn with her foot, she threw the *cochonnet* the regulation 6 to 10 paces and then shaped up to launch her first *boule*.

'Stand back everyone!' shouted Harry. 'We have countdown! 10, 9, 8, 7'

'Do you mind, Harry Birch?' cried Mavis, turning round to glare at him.

Forgetting the back-hand lob she'd intended, Mavis threw her *boule* open-handed high in the air. To her delight, it landed only a metre from the *cochonnet* but then, unrestrained by backspin, it rolled rapidly forward to leave the *piste* altogether and disappear under a bush.

'Tough luck, Mavis,' shouted Harry po-faced, 'so near and yet so far.'

'You put me off, you horrible man,' Mavis retorted. 'Bet you don't do any better.'

Harry strode confidently to the throwing circle. Before the others arrived, he had asked Monique to give him a little coaching. Bending at the knees, eyes focussed on the *cochonnet*, he sent his backhand lob sailing into the air and waited for the applause when it came down a foot from its target. Harry's moment of triumph was short-lived. His *boule* landed on a sharp stone and skittered away to stop a good three metres from the *cochonnet*.

'Just what you deserve,' shrieked Mavis gleefully.
'Sod's Law,' growled Harry, 'but at least mine stayed on the *piste*.'

Since lobbing had proved so ineffective, Betty decided on a different technique. Bending on one knee as if she were playing on grass, she prepared to bowl underhand to the ill-concealed derision of two onlookers who had been attracted by the shouts. Betty's aim and judgment of speed were impeccable: her *boule* lurched from left to right on the pebbly track and finally ended up nestling against the *cochonnet*. Arms raised, she acknowledged the cheers of Mavis, Penny and Joyce, following which she bowed graciously to the two spectators, now looking at each other in blank amazement.

'There's only one thing you can do now, Bert, shift it,' said Harry. Bert ambled forward and gave some thought to the situation. He then flexed his muscles, brought his right arm over his shoulder and hurled the *boule* as if he were putting the shot at the Olympic Games. Whether he under-estimated its weight or over-estimated his own strength, the *boule* failed miserably to get anywhere near the jack. Worse, it finished up blocking the way for a direct assault on Betty's winning *boule*. Harry groaned, muttered a curse and told Bert to try again – with a lob this time. Bert's second throw was an improvement on his first but only marginally. There were now two *boules* blocking the way as Harry came forward to save the day. To bomb or not to bomb, that was the question. In the end, he decided on a low trajectory volley: if he could land his *boule* beyond the two obstructions, he was in with a chance. There was nothing wrong with Harry's aim. Straight as a die, his *boule* flew over the two left by Bert. Sadly for Harry, it also flew over Betty's *boule* and didn't stop until it reached the long grass four metres beyond the *piste*. Harry raised his arms heavenwards, appealing for justice.

'Tough luck Harry,' shrilled Mavis, 'so near and yet so far.'

With one *boule* each to play, she and Betty went

into a huddle. Should they play safe and settle for one certain point or should they try for more. 'Let's go for it,' said Mavis. 'There's a gap of three metres between your *boule* and Harry's. I'll try to drop mine between them.'

There was silence this time as Mavis prepared to throw but when her *boule* scored a second point, loud cheers broke out from Penny and Joyce. Betty now thought discretion the better part of valour: better to play safe than risk losing a two point lead.

Harry put a brave face on the poor start of Bert and himself. They hadn't wanted to discourage the ladies in the first game. He confidently predicted a match winning score of 13 – 6, once his partner had learned how not to throw the *boules*.

Bert, too busy rubbing his upper right arm, didn't hear this remark.

'Think I've pulled a muscle, Harry. Maybe I'd better drop out. Daresay I'll be O.K. tomorrow. You couldn't spare me some of that arnica you rubbed on my leg, Monique? It worked wonders.'

Monique said she could but she didn't offer to apply it. As he walked off in the direction of the bar, Harry asked him to get one in for himself; he'd be along shortly as soon as he'd sized up the opposition they'd be facing in the play-off. Joyce decided to emulate Betty by bowling underarm but her *boule* veered well off course. Penny's attempt at a more orthodox lob was even less successful: instead of describing the graceful arc she'd intended before landing near the jack, her *boule* soared upwards almost vertically, landed two metres away and then spun back to within a metre of where she was standing. Bill and Syd thought this highly amusing but their own efforts were found equally entertaining by the seven or eight spectators who had now gathered round.

When all eight *boules* had been played, the four still remaining on the *piste* were so widely dispersed that Monique was called upon to adjudicate. After pacing to and fro several times, she awarded victory by the narrowest of margins to Bill but when Joyce begged leave to differ, Monique ran back to the hotel and returned with a tape measure. In the end, Joyce reluctantly conceded defeat; Bill had won by one centimetre.

'Nothing to beat there in the final,' said Harry to Mavis as they walked back to the hotel to get ready for dinner. 'They're rubbish. We'll win hands down, Bert and I.'

'Don't count your chickens,' retorted Mavis. 'You have to beat Betty and me first and you're two nil down, remember?'

LA MER DE GLACE

O.L. made sure no-one missed the 09.03 train next morning into Chamonix. She told Bert there was no time for his fourth cup of coffee; he should have got down earlier for breakfast. Penny was instructed to finish her second croissant on the way to the station and Joyce told that last minute visits to the toilet were out of the question.

Waiting on the platform with ten minutes to spare, Harry opened his i-pod to see if Gladys had replied to the e-mail he'd sent about their journey and safe arrival. What he read brought a wide grin to his face.

'I say, everyone, come and listen to this,' he shouted, 'I've just had an e-mail from Gladys.'

With everyone gathered round, Harry read out the e-mail.

'Glad to hear you all made it, although it wasn't exactly a smooth journey, was it! Just read a report in today's paper about Saturday's car crash in the High Street under the heading 'Mystery Man in Rescue Bid.' That's got to be Bert, hasn't it. You can't see his face on the photo and I don't recall him wearing a red anorak but I can make out his bald patch. Mrs Brenda Williams is anxious to thank him for rescuing her baby and herself and would appreciate any information about his identity. Good old Bert! Love to all. Gladys. P.S. Should I reveal his name?'

Harry was left in no doubt about the answer he should send back to Gladys. An emphatic 'yes' came from everyone with one exception. Bert envisged his name splashed over the papers, journalists pestering him for interviews and television cameras at his front door. Granted his pal Harry would have liked nothing better but no thanks, it wasn't for him.

'But couldn't you just let Gladys give your name to Mrs Williams?' persisted Mavis, 'She only wants to thank you.'

After some hesitation, Bert agreed on one condition: Gladys could give his name to Mrs Williams but on no account to the press. Harry shrugged his shoulders. What a wasted opportunity! As an eye-witness, he could have fleshed out the story of Bert's heroics – with himself in a supporting rôle. What's more, he could have heightened the drama by describing their race against time to get to the airport, Bert's return home to shower and change, the ruined anorak, the forgotten wallet and passport, the missed train, the speeding taxi. And it wouldn't have ended there. The local press would certainly have wanted to know about Thurston Ramblers' trip to Chamonix and Harry would gladly have supplied them with all the details and photos they could possibly have wished for.

In the train, Harry was strangely subdued but meeting Monique at the station and walking with her through Chamonix, he soon forgot about Bert's aversion to publicity. Now was the time to try out the phrases he'd already rehearsed before breakfast.

'*Combien de temps pour monter au Plan de l'Aiguille? C'est à quelle altitude? Un aller, c'est combien?*'

Monique congratulated him on his much improved accent and said the cable car took about ten minutes to get up to 2354 metres and a single ticket cost 12.50 euros. At first, he had difficulty understanding the figures which Monique made him repeat several times. When she finally approved of his pronunciation, he turned round in triumph to inform anyone within earshot that *le Plan de l'Aiguille est à deux mille trois cent cinquante-quatre mètres.*

'Really!' replied O.L. who already knew how high they were going and didn't have to add to Harry's triumph by asking for a translation. 'I can't wait to get up there.'

Queueing for tickets, Bert remembered that Mavis had talked about a Multipass which made cable-cars less expensive. Would they save much by buying one?

'No we wouldn't, Mavis replied. 'When I worked out the costs for the week, I realised a Multipass wouldn't be worth buying for most of us. Even if the *Aiguille du Midi* on the Free Day were included, the saving would be minimal. I don't think you'll be going up there on Wednesday, Bert?'

Bert assured her he had other plans for the Free Day as did Mike and Joe whose tour of the heliport with Monique's brother had been confirmed. Only O.L., Harry, Betty and Bill expressed definite interest in the *Aiguille du Midi:* the others would decide later.

Penny, who had only recently overcome her fear of flying, watched apprehensively as the cable-car slowly came down to dock. Among the dozen or so passengers who emerged were a goup of Japanese tourists rubbing their hands together for warmth, obviously relieved to have got down. With the summit temperature given as -10°, Penny was glad she was only going halfway. But how did it work she wanted to know.

Joe, who always seemed to understand how things worked, explained that it was all to do with counterbalance: the cable-car going up was counterbalanced by the cable-car coming down and there was a system of counterweights to maintain equilibrium if one cable-car were more heavily loaded than the other. The overhead cable to which the cable-car was attached was supported at intervals by huge pylons and driven by a powerful electric motor. It was a wonderful feat of engineering.

Once crammed inside the cabin with a full load of 70 passengers, Penny hoped the counterweights were in good working order; there wouldn't be anything like that number coming down at this time of day. Hemmed in on all sides, she was perfectly happy to forego the spectacular views of Chamonix below as they gained height. Among the 'ohs' and 'ahs' that came from people standing by the windows, she could hear uninhibited exclamations of delight from a high-pitched voice that could only belong to O.L. Harry would no doubt be too busy with his camera to tell her to tone it down.

Emerging from the *Plan de l'Aiguille* station, they were met by a cool breeze but the sun was shining and the visibility perfect as they walked down the rocky path to join the *Grand Balcon Nord* heading towards the *Mer de Glace*. More than a thousand metres below lay the valley of Chamonix backed by the jagged peaks of the *Aiguilles Rouges*. O.L, map in hand as she strode along, was so enraptured by the scene that she forgot to watch where she was putting her feet and stumbled several times. Harry couldn't resist wagging a finger.

'Now then, Olive, remember what your hero Mr Wainwright said, you can't look at the view and your feet at the same time.'

Running parallel to the valley and above the treeline, the stony, almost horizontal path crossed streams coming down from the glaciers above but presented no difficulty for the first two kilometers. Pausing at a fork, Monique announced that there was now a series of zigzags which would take them up 150 meters to the *Signal Forbes*. Here they would have breathtaking views over the *Mer de Glace* and the mountains surrounding it.

The climb took its toll on Joyce and Penny. Red-faced and sweating profusely they plodded on but soon lost sight of the others. Harry too was not on great form. To his dismay, he found himself struggling to keep pace with Bert. The fitness he'd displayed only a few weeks ago on Skiddaw, Helvellyn and Scafell Pike seemed to have deserted him. When he stopped abruptly, ostensibly to admire the view, Bert was not fooled.

'What's up, Harry? You look knackered. Run out of nuts and raisins, have you? If a Mars Bar would help, you can have one of mine.'

'Kind of you to offer, Bert, but no thanks. Maybe I had a glass too many of the red stuff last night at dinner. How's that pulled muscle in your bowling arm, by the way? If Monique's arnica didn't cure it, I'll give it a massage when we get to the top. Can't have you letting the side down again.'

O.L. was first to the top. Any hill to her was a

challenge, an obstacle to be overcome on a par with foul weather, a test of stamina and willpower. In the absence of a path, instinct would have driven her to take a direct line for the summit: here, given zigzags to follow and a derisory 150 meters of ascent, she had set off at a brisk pace to reach the top a good five minutes before the arrival of Joyce and Penny escorted by Harry.

Harry knew very well why he was struggling. It wasn't just down to over indulgence in wine and beer though that was doubtless a factor. Since leaving home, he hadn't done any of the exercise routines prescribed by his personal trainer. Nor, in the last few days, had he given a thought to the strict diet he'd followed doggedly over the past few months. Yesterday's raspberry tart swimming in cream was only one of the many gastronomic temptations he'd succumbed to since arriving in Chamonix. True, he had already proved his ability to keep pace with O.L. but he had yet to demonstrate his recenstly acquired fitness to Monique. Only after he'd done this, could he allow himself to enjoy the pleasures of rich food and copious drink. In the meanwhile, he would just have to restrain himself.

O.L. was in her seventh heaven. With her map spread out on a rock and orientated, she reeled off the names of peaks and glaciers she could identify, *les Drus, la Verte, les Grandes Jorasses, la Mer de Glace* and *le Glacier de Leschaux*. It wasn't until she paused for breath that Monique was able to get a word in.

'You know a lot of these mountains were first climbed by British *alpinistes* in the mid 19th century. On the map you will see some of their names, *Pointe Walker, Pointe Whymper* and *Pointe Young*.'

'I know,' cried O.L., 'I've read all about them. Whymper was the first to climb the *Aiguille Verte* and Young was the first to traverse the *Grandes Jorasses*. Then in the 1950s, there was Don Whillans, Joe Brown and Chris Bonington.'

'Not to mention Mike and me twenty years ago,' added Joe. 'First time we'd done any climbing in the Alps. Remember when we crossed the *Mer de Glace,* Mike, intending to do the *Aiguille du Moine?* Never made it, did we.'

'Not a couple of days I'm likely to forget, Joe. Making our way over a glacier, dodging crevasses was a new experience for us. On the other side, we got held up on those near vertical ladders at *Les Egralets*. Half way up, a young lad froze and his father made matters worse by shouting abuse at him. Then, when we finally reached the *Couvercle* hut, the heavens opened and we had to spend the night there.'

'Next morning, it was still raining and the visibility was down to about ten yards,' continued Joe, 'so we decided to abort. It wasn't easy finding our way back to the ladders and going down them in the wet was very tricky. Then we had to pick our way back over the glacier in fog which seemed to take for ever. We weren't half glad to get off the glacier that day!'

'I still remember the fug when we went into the hotel in *Montenvers*,' added Mike, 'it was like going into a Turkish Bath. There must have been a score of walkers and climbers, all as wet as ourselves, drying out in front of a big log fire.'

O.L. hung on their every word. Walking on ice,

dodging crevasses and climbing ladders was a challenge she would really enjoy. It would almost compensate for having to abandon her dream of climbing Mont Blanc.

'I presume we will be walking on the glacier today,' she asked Monique. 'I'm sure we would all relish the experience.'

'Well, actually, we're not going to walk **on** the glacier,' replied Monique, 'we're going to walk **under** it! When we get down to *Montenvers,* we can take the gondola to visit the grotto carved out of the ice underneath the glacier. I am sure everyone will enjoy that.'

Joyce and Penny clapped their hands, relieved to hear they would not be walking on the glacier and dodging crevasses but O.L. showed no great enthusiasm for visiting what was obviously a tourist attraction in the company of scores of day-trippers who had come up to *Montenvers* by train. Bert said he would like to see the grotto but what would it cost?

'Nothing you can't afford, Bert, you old skinflint,' replied Mavis who had visited the grotto last year. 'Anyway, you don't have to take the gondola: a twenty minute walk will bring you to the steps leading down to the grotto.'

'In that case,' interspersed O.L. shouldering her rucksack, 'we'll walk. We are walkers after all, are we not?'

'Not so fast, Olive,' cried Harry, 'we haven't climbed up to this glorious viewpoint to go straight down again. I've loads of photos to take. Would *mademoiselle* be kind enough to pose on that rock over there with *les Drus* in the background?'

More interested in food than photos, Bert thought it was picnic time. In the shop that morning, he had come across Joyce looking longingly at a melon. She had picked it up, told him it was ripe and juicy, but ruefully put it back, saying it was too heavy. Bert had then come up with a solution: if she would buy it, he would carry it. Naturally, he'd expect some recompense for porterage – say a third share. Joyce had beaten him down to a quarter share, bought the melon and Bert had carried up Now it was pay-back time and he couldn't wait to enjoy the fruit of his labour.

It took a while before picnic places were chosen to suit everyone. In the absence of trees, Penny, Joyce and Betty found a modicum of shade behind some rocks; Mike and Joe made for a vantage point looking down on the glacier while Syd and Bill settled down in a hollow which Bill considered ideal for a post-prandial siesta. O.L., accompanied by Mavis, headed off to climb a boulder which promised to give fine views of the *Grandes Jorasses* while Harry, with Monique in tow, went off to take photos.

'Fancy a slice of melon for starters, ladies?' cried Bert, 'A sweeter, juicier melon than this you've never tasted. Normal price 5 euros, special offer to you, 3 euros. If that's not a bargain, I don't know what is.'

'Of all the cheek,' exclaimed Joyce, 'you selling my melon!'

'Just joking, Joyce. Mind you, I've sweated blood carrying it up here so I think I've earned my quarter share. Now what we need is a flat rock to cut it up.'

Closely supervised by Joyce, Bert quartered the

melon, took his share, ate it voraciously, smacked his lips and then went off to join Syd and Bill. After making short work of a tin of *salade niçoise*, a wedge of *quiche lorraine* and an *éclair au chocolat*, washed down with a can of lager, Bert felt at peace with the world and stretched out to follow the example of Syd and Bill, already in the land of Nod. It wasn't long before his peace was shattered by a low rumbling growl which rose to a crescendo before ending abruptly in a loud snort. To his amazement, Syd's snoring had no effect on Bill who, it turned out, had taken the precaution of wearing ear plugs, but Bert found it unbearable and scurried off to seek peace elsewhere.

When the time came for Monique to gather the group together, she had no difficulty locating Syd and Bill but it took a search party ten minutes to find Bert before they could begin the 300 metre descent to the *Mer de Glace*. O.L's displeasure at the delay reached boiling point when, half way down, Bert realised he'd forgotten his stick.

'Really, Bert, I wish you'd get your act together,' she exclaimed. 'I suggest you leave your stick where it is and buy yourself another one. You've caused us enough delay as it is.'

'I can't do that! It's the stick Gladys lent me,' came Bert's anguished reply, 'I'll have to go back for it. You don't have to wait for me. I'll catch you up at the bottom.'

'Hang on, Bert,' said Harry, 'we can't have you getting lost as well as Gladys's stick. I'll go back up with you. Mind you, it'll cost you a couple of beers when we get to the hotel.'

Bert nodded as they started the climb back up the

zig-zags, leaving the others to continue their descent to *Montenvers*. In spite of the cool air coming up from the glacier, Penny and Joyce found the heat oppressive. Noticing that they were perspiring freely, Monique called for a pause.

'You know it's not enough to apply sun-cream: you must also drink plenty of water, even if you don't feel thirsty. Otherwise, like Mike said, you will be shutting the stable door after the 'orse 'as bolted it. 'Ave I got it right, Mavis?'

'Very nearly, Monique, except that you've forgotten 'bolt' here means 'to run away' not 'lock' so you don't need 'it' at the end. I've got plenty of water, by the way, if anyone's run short.'

Joyce had already finished the half litre bottle she'd brought and was glad to accept more. Looking down on the *Mer de Glace*, she asked Monique about the curved lines pointing downwards on the surface of the ice: they looked like waves on the sea.

'They are caused by the movement of the glacier.' Monique replied. 'You know glaciers are always moving; they advance from their source and retreat from their base. How fast depends on things like gradient, snowfall and temperature.'

'But why the curved lines?' asked Betty.

Monique explained that the lines curved downwards because the glacier moved more quickly in the middle than at the edges. The distance between the lines generally showed how far the ice had advanced in a year. Where a glacier narrowed at a bend, the pressure increased so much that huge blocks of ice called *seracs* were forced upwards.

They would be walking quite close to *seracs* when they went to *le glacier du Tour* on Thursday.

Harry and Bert, complete with stick, caught them up just as they were approaching *Montenvers*. A train had just arrived and all the tables on the terrace outside the hotel were occupied by tourists seeking shade and refreshment under the brightly coloured parasols. Harry shrugged his shoulders but when he said he didn't mind if they had to wait five minutes for a free table, O.L. announced that she herself had no intention of hanging about in all that noise and bustle for one minute, let alone five. If Monique would kindly indicate the path, she would set off at once to visit the ice grotto.

Monique looked around to gauge the general opinion. It seemed that Harry was in a minority of one. Even Bert appeared to side with O.L.

'Suppose we wait for drinks until after the visit, 'Arry?' she asked, smiling sweetly. 'There will be plenty of room here then and you will enjoy your beer even more after you've climbed back up the 400 steps from the cave.'

Harry graciously accepted defeat but Penny was alarmed to hear about so many steps.

'No pain, no gain, Penny my love,' said Harry. 'It's not everyday you get the chance to see inside a glacier. When you're sweating down those steps, just think how lovely and cool you'll be inside.'

'Actually,' added Mavis, 'you might be glad of a sweater. You'll certainly need to put your anorak on and wear a hat.'

On the 20 minute walk alongside the glacier, Penny

forgot about the steps when she saw a large bird circling high above on the thermals.

'Monique,' she shouted, getting out her binoculars, 'that bird, I think it's a golden eagle. It's huge! It must have a wingspan of two metres! I can see the grey patch on its wedge-shaped tail. What do you think?'

Everyone stopped as Monique focussed on the bird, confirmed Penny's opinion and passed her binoculars round the group.

'That's a first for me, Penny,' enthused Joe, 'I know there's a pair nesting in the Lake District but I've never been lucky enough to see them.'

It was a first for them all except Penny and Monique but O.L.'s interest was short-lived. She'd had enough after two or three minutes and when no-one showed any desire to move on, she called out in exasperation:

'Now we've seen it, what are we waiting for? It's only going round in circles.'

Penny found the steps easier than she'd feared. On the way down, she was interested by the marks showing how much the glacier had shrunk over the past years, proof, she thought, of global warming.

Water dripping from the roof at the entrance to the tunnel made everyone put on anoraks and hats but the drop in temperature came as a relief. What impressed Betty in particular was the translucent, turquoise ice, as smooth as marble: she thought the coloured lights gave a surreal effect to the sculptures in the grotto. O.L. was most attracted by the sight of water cascading down crevasses while Harry and Bert were delighted to have their photos taken on the way out next to a large St Bernard dog.

'An experience not to be missed' was the general verdict as they emerged into strong sunlight and took off anoraks. Pleased they had enjoyed the visit, Monique said that it took three months every year to renovate the grotto and carve the ice sculptures.

Aiming to make up for the exercises he'd neglected in the past few days, Harry climbed determinedly the 400 steps close on the heels of O.L. and well ahead of the pack.

At the top, dripping with sweat, he pulled off his shirt, stood bolt upright, put his hands on his hips and began deep breathing exercises. Not content with this, he continued with twelve knees bends and as many press-ups. Perched on a rock, O.L. looked on in amazement and not a little admiration. Was this the same Harry Birch she'd seen plodding laboriously up the zig-zags with Penny and Joyce only a few hours ago?

'Just loosening up a bit,' called Harry, putting on his shirt. 'Got to keep the muscles toned and the flab down.'

'I must say I'm impressed,' replied O.L. 'You'll be giving up beer next.'

'That, Olive, is asking too much. But now you mention it, I've a thirst like a dredger and I can't wait to quench it, courtesy of my friend Bert here, who I see has just arrived.'

Bert took the hint when they got back to the hotel in *Montenvers*. He hadn't seen Harry exercising but he had seen how quickly he'd climbed up from the cave.

'Pushing your luck there, weren't you, Harry, flying up those steps like a bat out of hell? Not trying to prove something, were you? At your age, you should be slowing down not speeding up.'

'He was proving there's life in the old dog yet, weren't you Harry,' added Mavis, winking at Monique.

'But 'Arry is not an old dog: 'e is a middle aged dog. 'Ees that not so, 'Arry?'

'You could say that, Monique. Or you could say 'e's in the prime of life.' Of the two, I prefer the latter. Think of me as a man at his peak.'

'So from now on, it's downhill all the way, right Harry?'

'Wrong, Joyce. Reaching one's peak doesn't mean an immediate descent. Think of Ingleborough: it may be called a peak but once you're on the top, what have you got? A plateau! A very wide plateau! Which is exactly where I propose to stay now that I'm at my peak. Come to think of it, we have among us a shining example. I refer, of course, to our esteemed president. If I may say so, Olive, you must have reached your peak some years ago. The remarkable thing is you're still on the plateau. Indeed, far from going downhill, you are still looking for more hills to climb! Ladies and gentlemen, I ask you to raise your glasses to our evergreen and indestructible president, long may she reign over us.'

Monique's loud cry 'Vive la présidente!' caused a stir on the terrace. Waiters stopped in their tracks and customers craned their necks to see which *présidente* they had in their midst. Presented with a captive audience, Harry burst into song to conduct a spirited rendering of 'For she's a jolly good fellow.' Not content with this, he then called for three cheers, inviting the spectators to join in.

O.L. couldn't believe her ears. Harry Birch singing her praises? The same Harry Birch who had been a thorn in her flesh ever since his election to the committee? He was exaggerating of course, over-acting in his usual flamboyant style but all the same, she felt gratified. Rising to acknowledge the applause, she thanked Harry for his kind if unexpected tribute. She aimed to stay at her peak for some years to come and hoped Harry would do the same. In view of his transformation in the past months, she didn't see why not.

'Well it's downhill all the way from here for all of us, I'm pleased to say,' interposed Bert. 'How long will it take, Monique?'

Monique said they had a descent of 830 metres to get back to the hotel. It was an easy track and would take them about two hours. Taking the train down in twenty minutes was a possibility but she assumed they would all prefer to walk, would they not? When O.L. immediately assured her that they all, without a doubt, would prefer to walk down, Harry raised an eyebrow. He'd meant his cry of 'long may she reign over us' to be taken humourously, not literally. Yet here she was riding roughshod over everyone, yet again.

'Not sure everyone would agree with you there, Olive,' he cried. 'It's just possible that Joyce and Penny might prefer to take the train, Bert too, I shouldn't wonder – though he might be put off by the fare of 19€'

When Bert replied that he'd have to be on crutches to pay that much, Joyce and Penny went into a huddle before finally declaring that although they were tired, they were not tired enough to part with 19€. All the same, they appreciated being given the option. To O.L.'s dismay, Joe announced that he and Mike were also tempted to take the train, not because they were tired but because they were both train enthusiasts.

'It's a fantastic feat of engineering,' said Joe, 'building a rack and pinion railway in terrain like this. It's just over five kilometres long and the gradient in places is 22%. When you think it was built in 1908, it's an amazing achievement. What do you think, Mike?'

'I'd like to ride up as well as down,' was Mike's opinion. 'What about doing that on the free day if we've time after visiting the heliport with Monique's brother?'

When Joe agreed, Monique said it was time to start the descent. The track through the trees was wide and stony in parts but they would be in shade. If Joyce and Penny felt like a rest, there was a café half way down. O.L. needed no such incentive. Going into overdrive, she was soon out of sight but at least had the good sense to wait at the café where the track forked. Last to arrive were Joyce and Penny, escorted by Harry. Bert took the view that it was Joyce and Penny who were escorting Harry and offered them his congratulations.

'Thought you'd gone back for the train, Harry. You look a bit under the weather. Could be a case of burn-out. Rushing up those steps like a madman was asking for trouble. You've got to learn to pace yourself, like Monique here. She looks as fresh as a daisy.'

'You are right, Bert,' added Monique. 'In the mountains, we never rush. We 'ave a saying *qui veut voyager loin, ménage sa monture.* 'Ow you say that in English, Mavis?'

'You should look after your horse if you've a long way to go,' replied Mavis.

'Just what you need, right now, Harry,' cried Bert, 'a horse to get you down!'

'A horse, a horse,' exclaimed Harry, 'my kingdom for a horse! And while we're at it, a sedan chair for my good friend Bert whose condition, I fear, is much worse than my own.'

Monique was puzzled by these exchanges of banter.

''Arry and Bert are always mocking each other,' she whispered to Mavis, 'they don't sound like good friends at all.'

'Oh they're good friends all right. Big buddies in fact – I think you would say *copains comme cochons.* They've known each other since primary school. They like nothing better than taking the mickey out of each other. Don't take them seriously: they do it for laughs.'

''Arry is a funny man but I don't see Olive laughing at his jokes: she is very serious, is she not?'

'They're like chalk and cheese, those two. They used to be at daggers drawn but now they both have a grudging respect for each other. Actually, I think our club needs them both.'

Harry would gladly have paused at the café for rest and refreshment but neither Joyce nor Penny expressed any desire to stop when Monique said they were behind schedule and wouldn't get back to the hotel before 6 o'clock.

'Looks like we'll have to postpone our unfinished *boules* match tonight, Mavis,' said Harry. 'By the time we've showered and you and Betty have got spruced up, they'll just about be serving dinner.'

'Very convenient for you, I must say,' retorted

Mavis. 'You look shattered. If we played tonight, we'd polish you off in no time.'

On the walk down to the hotel, Harry concealed his fatigue as best he could but after climbing the stairs to his room, pulling off his boots and forcing himself to shower, he stretched out on his bed and promptly fell asleep. When he appeared for dinner just as the soup was being served, he was greeted by an ironic round of applause, led by his good friend Bert.

LE LAC BLANC

Harry made up for his late arrival for dinner by being first down for breakfast. He had slept like a log, been up since 6, completed his exercise routine and sent an e-mail to Gladys saying she could reveal Bert's name to Mrs Williams provided the press were not informed.

Wearing pale blue shorts and a silk shirt adorned with highly coloured exotic flowers, he expected sardonic comments from Bert and a disapproving frown from O.L. but when Mavis, one of his fan club, said all he needed to complete the picture was a hula hoop, he was rather hurt. Worse was to follow when Joyce declared he reminded her of a man selling ice-cream on the beach at Torremolinos.

Bert covered his eyes in mock horror and hoped Harry would have the decency to walk behind him. Seeing that poncy silk shirt in front of him would put him off his food all day.

'That'll be the day, when you're off your food,' replied Harry forcing a laugh, 'and go easy with those stewed apricots, they're supposed to be for all of us.'

During breakfast, Harry was not his usual jovial self. Far from attracting undiluted admiration, his expensive silk shirt had met with derision. Syd's casual remark that he'd seen a similar shirt on a model in an Oxfam shop window did nothing to improve his mood.

It was the arrival of Monique after breakfast which restored his good spirits.

'*Bonjour tout le monde, j'arrive avec le soleil,*' she cried gaily before suddenly catching sight of Harry. '*Arry, quelle transformation! J'aime bien ta belle chemise.* So colourful! And your blue shorts! You are very chic today.'

'Now there speaks a lady of excellent taste,' exclaimed Harry triumphantly. '*Merci, mademoiselle, merci mille fois.* And may I say, in return, how pretty you look in your red shorts and green top. We must have our photo taken together when we get to the lake.'

Monique spread her map on a table in the garden to talk about the day's walk.

'Today we walk on the other side of the valley below *les Aiguilles Rouges*. Opposite us, we shall have stunning views of *la Mer de Glace* and *le Massif du Mont-Blanc*. It's a circular walk, shorter than yesterday, roughly 4 hours long with about 475 metres of climbing.'

'Ooh,' cried Joyce, 'that's a lot more climbing than we did yesterday.'

Monique agreed but pointed out that it was no more than they had done on Monday. Besides, the descent would be less than half as long as what they did yesterday.

'You'll be glad about that, Harry,' chipped in Bert, 'You were sleepwalking coming down from the *Mer de Glace* yesterday. I should take it easy today if I were you. Don't worry if you lag too far behind and get lost: we'd spot that shirt a mile away – in fog!'

'Exactly what I thought when I bought it, Bert. Not only is it a thing of beauty, as Monique has just testified, it is also very practical. Think how many lives would be saved if walkers in distress could be so easily spotted. Now in your case, I'm afraid you'd be doomed: you're so well camouflaged you'd never be seen in the mountains. Come to think of it, your shiny pate might help on a sunny day ... especially if you applied a coat of luminous paint.'

Bert grinned. With the score at one all and honours even, Mavis asked if they would now kindly allow Monique to continue.

'Our walk starts from *La Flégère* at 1877 metres and the cable-car costs 13.50€ return. It will take us about two hours to get up *Le Lac Blanc*. We'll picnic by the lakeside. It is a very beautiful place and there is a refuge serving drinks and snacks. After our picnic, we take a path down past the five *Lacs des Chéserys* to meet the *Grand Balcon Sud*, part of *Le Tour du Mont-Blanc*, to return to *La Flégère.*'

'What about the flora and fauna, Monique?' asked Mavis. 'When you took me there last year, the flowers were magnificent and I remember how much we enjoyed watching the choughs and spotting the marmots.'

'Oh yes!' cried Monique, 'we're sure to see choughs at *le Lac Blanc* and marmots on our way down to *Chéserys* this afternoon. It's a pity the rhodenrons will no longer be in flower but there will be plenty of other flowers to see that love the south-facing slopes.'

'Rhododendrons?' queried Betty. 'I didn't expect to see those in the mountains.'

Mavis explained that dwarf rhododendrons, growing no higher than a foot, were very much at home in the Alps. They often colonised hillsides as big as football pitches. In late June or July, their mass of pinky red flowers was a glorious sight.

'Sounds most attractive,' interrupted O.L., 'but we won't see flowers or marmots by standing here. I suggest we get moving. Everybody got enough water? Applied plenty of sun cream, Joyce and Penny?'

'Yes, Olive, thank you very much, we're smothered in it,' Joyce replied. 'But I think it's Harry you should be asking. I bet his knees haven't seen the light of day since he was a nipper.'

'Very true, Joyce my love. Today is a very special occasion. I trust your first sighting of my knees and shapely calves has given you a little *frisson*. In return, I look forward to seeing you taking a dip in the lake when we get there. You have brought your bikini, I hope.'

'No I haven't,' retorted Joyce, 'but if I see you fully immersed, I'll go in without it.'

'You're on safe ground there, Joyce,' cried Bert. 'He might immerse his big toe if there's a heated paddling pool up there but that's as far as he'll go.'

O.L. had had enough of this repartee. Striding ahead of Monique, she was already in the queue at the cable car station when the others arrived.

'I see we could go higher than *La Flégère*,' she called out to Monique. 'We could go up to *L'Index* at 2385 metres and walk across to *le Lac Blanc* from there. We would have marvellous views all the way of the *Mont-Blanc massif*.'

'It's possible,' called back Monique, not very enthusiasticallly. 'Just get a return ticket for *La Flégère* and we'll decide when we get there.'

'She's at it again, trying to rule the roost,' muttered

Harry to Mavis. 'You can be sure Monique's already considered going higher and decided against it.'

Emerging from the cable car, Monique gathered the group together and pointed to the continuously revolving chair-lift going up to l'*Index* 500 metres higher. Ahead of them, three people climbed in a chair, pulled down the tubular frame and soared upwards.

'I'm not going up in one of those,' shrieked Joyce. 'Dangling in the air like that! The very thought of it makes me feel ill.'

When Penny said she couldn't face the chair-lift either, a scenario Monique had anticipated, O.L shrugged her shoulders in disbelief. Intolerant of human frailty at the best of times, she had no patience with people who, in her opinion, allowed imaginary fears and phobias to control their lives.

'If that's the case,' she snapped, 'we'll walk up.'

'I don't think that is a very good idea Olive,' interposed Monique. 'It would take us too long. As you know, a group's progress depends on the speed of its slowest walker. Besides, the path to *l'Index* is quite steep and stony and on the *traversée* to *le Lac Blanc* there is some scrambling over rocks.'

'Sounds like a challenge,' cried O.L. brightening up. 'What do you say, Mike and Joe? I'm up for it if you are. We could rejoin the others at the *Lac Blanc.*'

'But you would get there an hour after us if you walked up to *l'Index,*' pointed out Monique. 'If you took the chair-lift, we would all arrive at the same time, more or less.'

Mike and Joe were both interested in going higher

but were more concerned than O.L about the others having to wait for them at the lake if they walked up.

'Very well,' replied O..L grudgingly, 'we'll take the chair-lift. I'll get the tickets.'

As they became airborne, O.L. sandwiched between Mike and Joe, Harry took a photo and shouted *bon voyage*. He had always suspected that O.L. would want to deviate from the programme suggested by Monique but as long as she wasn't allowed to bulldoze everyone else into following her, she was welcome to do her own thing.

After a short descent, the wide, stony track began zigzagging its way up past the *Lac de la Flégère* at 2027 metres. Here Monique called a halt to point out the mountains and glaciers of the *Mont-Blanc Massif* on the opposite side of the valley. Ahead of them rose the jagged peaks of the *Aiguilles Rouges*, topped by the *Aiguille du Belvédère* at 2965 metres.

'Must say it beats Snowdonia, Syd,' murmured Bill. 'the sky-line all round is superb.'

'I could sit here all day,' declared Penny, 'just soaking up the views.'

'Don't get too comfortable, Penny dear,' called Harry. 'Monique's just told me we've still got an hour's climbing to do. Have another slurp of water and think of the choughs you'll see at the *Lac Blanc.* If you're flagging, I'm sure Bert will carry your rucksack if you ask him nicely.'

'And offer to buy him a beer at the refuge,' added Joyce.

'I'll do it for nothing if Penny lends me her

sunglasses,' cried Bert. 'Anything to tone down that shirt of Harry's. He keeps getting in front of me. It's like following a disco with all its coloured lights flashing.'

Penny said she was quite capable of carrying her own rucksack but offered Bert her sunglasses if he offered to buy her a coffee at the refuge. Bert readily agreed to this saying he'd never struck a better bargain in his life.

It was obvious that Joyce and Penny were struggling as the track narrowed and became steeper. Waiting for them to catch up, Bill looked back to see them chattering away like magpies as they plodded uphill.

'I'll never understand women,' he announced. 'They'll be breathless when they get here but they always seem to have enough breath to chat when they're walking; uphill, downhill or on the flat, it doesn't make any difference.'

'Can't think what they have to talk about,' commented Syd, himself a man of few words. 'It's a mystery to me. Mind you, my wife's just the same. When she and her pal next door get together, they'll talk till the cows come home.'

Monique had followed the gist of these exchanges but couldn't understand the connection between Syd's talkative wife and neighbour and cows coming home. When Mavis explained that it meant they would talk for ever, she burst into laughter.

'We would say they were *moulins à paroles* who would chatter *jusqu'au jour où les poules auront des dents*. But it's not only women who talk non-stop!'

'Too true,' added Bert. 'When Harry gets on his soapbox, he's a right windbag.'

Harry's riposte was drowned by Mavis's shout to Joyce and Penny.

'Hey, girls, Bill wants to know how you manage to chat all the time coming uphill and Syd wants to know what you find to talk about.'

'Tell them to mind their own business,' shouted back Joyce. 'We enjoy a good natter, don't we, Penny? That's what keeps us going; stops us thinking about our aching legs.'

'Well now you've caught us up at last, we'll push on,' cried Harry mischievously.

'You can push on if you like, Harry Birch, but Joyce and I are staying put for the next five minutes,' exclaimed Penny. 'We've run out of breath.'

'Now there you surprise me, Penny, I didn't think that was possible,' said Harry, resuming his seat on a rocky outcrop, 'but there's no shade here. We don't want to risk sunburn. How far to go, Monique?'

When Monique said they were only about ten minutes walk from the lake and the path levelled out, Penny and Joyce agreed to postpone their rest. The climb from *La Flégère* had taken longer than anticipated and Monique was sure that O.L., Mike and Joe would already have arrived.

Seeing the lake backed by mountain peaks rejuvenated Joyce and Penny. What rejuvenated Bert was the sight of the refuge overlooking the lake.

'Fancy an aperitif, Harry?' he called.

'Now you mention it, Bert, I don't mind if I do. One condition though. I insist you take off those dark glasses. You look like a Chicago gangster.'

'There they are!' cried Mavis, 'By that big boulder. I don't believe it: O.L.'s paddling in the lake!'

While Harry and Bert made their way to the refuge, the others went to join Mike and Joe, already half way through their picnics. O.L. came out of the water to greet them, her face wreathed in smiles. She'd had a splendid walk from *l'Index*, enjoyed scrambling over the rocks, been thrilled by fabulous views across the valley and seen three chamois! They were too far off to photograph but clearly visible through binoculars. She'd eaten her picnic, found the ice-cold water very refreshing and couldn't wait to start the second leg of the walk.

'Hang on Olive,' cried Mavis, 'we've only just got here. Why don't you have a nice little siesta? We'll wake you up when we're ready to go.'

'Siesta? Siesta? I haven't come up here to sleep!' exclaimed O.L. 'I'll have a walk round the lake while you're eating.'

It was only then that she realised that Harry and Bert were missing. Informed by Bill that they'd stopped at the refuge, she snorted, said she might have guessed and stalked off.

The choughs that Monique had mentioned were not slow to appear, attracted by the prospect of free food. Penny in particular was delighted with their aerial acrobatics.

'Aren't they agile!' she cried, 'turning, twisting and diving. And they're so handsome with their yellow beaks, red legs and glossy black plumage!'

'They certainly earn their crumbs, putting on a display like that,' added Mavis.

When Harry and Bert came down to the lake side, the choughs had been well fed. Most had already left to circle another group of picnickers but of the few remaining, one obligingly posed on a rock to be photographed by Harry two yards away.

'I bet he'd enjoy your chicken sandwich, Bert,' he whispered. 'Hold out your arm and see if he'll eat out of your hand. I'll hide behind that rock and take the photo.'

'Nay Harry,' protested Bert, 'I didn't buy this chicken sandwich to feed birds. He'll have to make do with this bit of cheese I've got left over from yesterday.'

Bert stood motionless for two minutes, arm outstretched, but the chough was unimpressed by the cheese and flew off in search of more appetising titbits elsewhere.

'You could have offered it a bit of chicken, you greedy beggar,' cried Penny, 'And don't forget the coffee you owe me.'

'All in good time, Penny. After we've finished eating and had a little nap, I won't forget to buy you a coffee.' replied Bert.

When O.L. returned from her tour of the lake, she was dismayed to find everyone sprawled out fast asleep. Her first thought was to wake up Monique and ask when they were leaving but in the end she decided to have a coffee at the refuge.and write a postcard to her friend Gladys. She would chose one showing chamois.

Harry did not sleep for long. Wakened by Syd's snoring and feeling hot and sweaty, he toyed with the possibility of following O.L.'s example and paddling in the lake but quickly rejected that idea after testing the temperature of the water with his hand. As he straightened up, he was startled to hear a voice shouting his name.

''Arry, 'Arry, come and join me! The water is lovely.'

Harry could hardly believe his eyes. To him the water was painfully cold and there was Monique, not only fully immersed but apparently enjoying her swim..

'Some other time, Monique,' he called back. 'Pity I left my trunks in the hotel.'

Roused by the shouts, the others lined the shore to applaud Monique as she swam across the lake. On rejoining them, she said she was used to swimming in mountain lakes and didn't find the water cold at all.

Sitting on the terrace outside the refuge, O.L. had seen Monique in the lake and was full of admiration for her spirit: had she herself been a little younger, she would have gone in as well, costume or not, just to show the flag. When the others joined her, she put on her rucksack, assuming they were about to set off on the next leg of their walk.

'Not so fast, Olive, Bert's buying me a coffee,' cried Penny. 'It's a first!'

'And probably the last,' added Harry, 'unless you can strike another bargain with him like washing his socks.'

'I'd want more than a coffee for that,' retorted Penny. 'A glass of champagne, at least.'

Monique called them together after everyone had finished coffee. They now had a descent of 200 metres to meet the *Grand Balcon/TMB* path. It wasn't a steep descent but there was a little obstacle to negotiate, a *passage équipé*.

'It's just a ladder to go down, only about four or five metres long and there are rails to hold,' she explained. 'It's nothing to worry about but I thought I'd tell you before we get there.'

Joyce and Penny exchanged worried looks but when they arrived at the edge of the cliff, their frowns deepened. It didn't help when O.L., first to go down, told them they were making a fuss about nothing; it was just like going backwards down a stile.

'I've never gone down a stile as high as this,' cried Joyce. 'Is there no way round it?'

When Monique shook her head, Mike stepped forward. He had dealt with similar situations during his service in the police force.

'I'll go first, just below you, and talk you down. Give your rucksack and stick to Joe. Hold the rails on each side and I'll plant your feet, one at a time, on the next rung. Don't look down. Relax and we'll make it in no time. Then I'll come back up for Penny.'

Encouraged by Mike's confident tone and his practical advice, Joyce slowly worked her way down the ladder to collapse in a heap at the bottom. Her legs, she said, were like jelly. When Penny joined her, Harry led a round of applause and Monique suggested a five minute halt to allow them to recover.

It was during the pause that a shrill whistling was heard.

'Marmot,' cried Mavis, getting out her binoculars. 'Over there, by those rocks. He's standing on his hind legs near his burrow. He knows we're here and he's whistling to warn the others.'

'If we keep quiet and don't move, he'll stay there long enough for us to take photos,' whispered Monique.

Harry needed no prompting. Not content with long-range shots, he was edging forward for a close-up when he stumbled over a rock and the marmot promptly disappeared down its burrow.

'Pushing your luck, there, Harry,' called Bert. 'You'd have done better hanging back. He obviously couldn't stand the sight of that psychedelic shirt you're wearing.'

'Not so, Bert,' retorted Harry, 'that marmot was so impressed by my floral shirt that he couldn't wait to tell his mates about it. They'll all be popping up now to take a look.'

Monique was sure they would hear and see more marmots as they walked down past the *Lacs de Chéserys* but she didn't really think they'd be much interested in Harry's shirt. At this time of year, what concerned them most was putting on enough fat to last them through the winter months when they hibernated.

Penny and Joyce, in particular good spirits after overcoming their fear of heights, were delighted by the profusion of flowers on the south facing grassy slopes and alongside the stony path. Among those they could recognise were brilliant blue gentian, pink, gold-centred asters and white anemones. Monique was able to identify others but there were frequent pauses for Mavis to consult her illustrated book of alpine flowers. Harry made the most of these stops to take close-ups but O.L. got increasingly impatient as the group strayed from the path and became more and more dispersed. In the end, she strode over to Mavis and beckoned her aside.

'Don't you think we've done enough botanizing for one day? We must have been here twenty minutes. I reckon it'll take us an hour and a half at our speed to get back to *La Flégère*. I think you should have a word with Monique: she must have forgotten that the last cable-car down is at 5 o'clock. I would be quite happy to go down on foot but I don't suppose some members of our group would be any too pleased at the prospect of another two hours walking, even if it is downhill.'

Monique had not forgotten. She assured Mavis they were in good time but all the same, thought it was time to move on. They would soon join the *Grand Balcon Sud* which formed part of the prestigious *Tour du Mont-Blanc*. Then there was a gradual descent with spectacular views ahead of the Chamonix Needles and Mont-Blanc itself.

In spite of her frustration at the delays – the siestas and coffee stop at the *Lac Blanc*, the hold up at the ladder and the time spent botanizing – O.L. was well satisfied with the day's outing and the last lap was the icing on the cake. If this section was typical of the *Tour du Mont-Blanc*, she resolved there and then to return next year to complete it. If she couldn't find anyone of like mind, she'd be quite happy doing it solo. There would be no need to hire a guide; she would manage perfectly well with the English version of the topoguide . What a way to celebrate her seventy-fifth birthday!

Still beaming at this prospect when they arrived at the cable-car station with half an hour to spare, she didn't object to Harry's proposal to take refreshment.

'You're looking very pleased with life, Olive,'

exclaimed Harry, offering her a chair at his table next to Monique. 'You look as if you've won the lottery.'

'That's the last thing I'd want!' cried O.L. 'From what I've read, lottery winners usually end up a lot less pleased with life than they were before.'

'Couldn't agree more,' chimed in Mike. 'The happiest people I've ever come across were the ones who had virtually nothing: in Nepal, for instance, I've never seen so many smiling faces. They have their problems no doubt, but they never look stressed or depressed.'

'That's to do with living close to nature in the mountains,' declared O.L. 'Here, for example, how could anyone feel stressed or depressed in surroundings like these? I recall Mr Wainwright saying one could even forget a raging toothache on the top of Haystacks in the Lake District. Personally, with views like this to contemplate, I could happily sit here until the sun goes down.'

'You'd miss the last cable-car, if you did,' pointed out Mavis.

'And your evening meal!' added Bert.

'It wouldn't harm me, or you for that matter, to miss a meal,' retorted O.L, 'and as for walking down, I find the idea very attractive. Anyone care to join me?'

'I wouldn't want to miss the evening meal but I'd enjoy walking down,' replied Mike. 'If we set off now, we could be back in time for the meal.'

When Joe agreed, all three took the track downhill. Monique was full of admiration for O.L.

'I hope I am as fit as Olive when I am an old lady,' she confided to Mavis.

'Me too,' said Mavis, 'but don't let her hear you

calling her an old lady: she's very sensitive about her age. She stopped counting when she reached forty.'

'Just like Harry,' interposed Bert. 'But he's gone one better than O.L. He doesn't just stick on forty: he subtracts a year evey birthday. Getting on for your second childhood now, aren't you Harry? I seem to remember you wearing a shirt like that when we were in the primary school together.'

'Correct, Bert,' cried Harry. 'Me, I get younger every day. In the company of these charming ladies, I feel about twenty. It's all in the mind you know: one's as young as one feels. I'll give you a few tips on rejuvenation, if you like. For a start, you could throw away that woolly bonnet you've worn for twenty years or more: we should have cremated it with your prehistoric anorak. Then you could get get rid of the scruffy old bags you're wearing before they finally give up the ghost. A decent shave with a new razor blade wouldn't come amiss either.'

'All right Harry,' interrupted Mavis, 'I think you've levelled the scores. Suppose we head for the cable-car now. Remember it's a two hour walk down if we miss it.'

Strolling back to the hotel from the lower station, Betty asked Harry and Bert if they felt fit enough to resume their unfinished game of *boules.*

'On the supposition that my elderly friend here doesn't feel the need for a nap,' Harry replied, 'and that we can count on the good offices of Monique to ensure fair play, I think we could stipulate a resumption of hostilities at half past six after a leisurely shower, a change of shirt and a call at the bar.'

Bert nodded saying he was relieved to hear that

Harry would be changing his shirt; not, he hoped, for another like it or he'd have to borrow Penny's sunglasses again.

When the match resumed, Bert surprised everyone, himself included, by winning the two points needed to level the score at two all. Harry was cock-a-hoop.

'Bert,' he exclaimed giving him a hug, 'you're a star. Remind me to buy you a beer when we get back to the bar. On present form, we'll be back there in no time.'

Harry's optimism was short-lived when Bert's early promise faded rapidly. If he sent his *boules* in the right direction, they either came to a stop well in front of the *cochonnet* or went sailing on well beyond it. His own performance was little better. Betty, on the other hand, who persisted in bowling underarm, consistently managed to place her *boules* within two feet of the target.

With the score at 10 – 5 against them, Harry drew Bert aside to suggest he follow Betty's example and bowl underarm. Bert didn't take kindly to this idea. Bowling underarm might be acceptable for ladies but for men it would be demeaning, like serving underarm in a tennis match.

'Maybe,' replied Harry, 'but it would be better than serving double faults all the time. At least you'd be in with a chance.'

Bert reluctantly agreed to give it a try. His first attempts were no better than before but as his direction and length improved, he began to win points and the score gradually levelled to 11 all. With only two more points needed for either side to claim victory, Bert rolled his first *boule* to within an inch of the jack. Mavis tried to shift it but missed by a whisker, her *boule* coming to rest a metre from Bert's. Betty's *boule* finished up near Mavis's but when Harry's lob landed very close to hers, Monique was called on to adjudicate. Her verdict, in favour of Harry by a centimetre, was loudly applauded by Bert.

'We've got the two points we need as things stand,' he exclaimed. 'If they don't do any better next round, we've won!'

Mavis told him not to count his chickens. Taking careful aim, she sent her *boule* high into the air to land between Harry's and the jack, reducing the deficit to one point. Betty then aimed to dislodge Bert's winning *boule* but her low trajectory volley, well off target, finished up in the long grass.

Harry and Bert were now faced with a tactical decision. Harry spelled out their three options: they could defend their one point lead by playing safe; they could try to deprive Mavis of her second place – and win the match – or they could attempt to dislodge Mavis's *boule* to leave Harry in second place – and win the match.

Maintaining that a bird in the hand was worth two in the bush, Bert made no attempt to score or to dislodge Mavis's *boule*. No way was he going to run the risk of dislodging his own *boule* only an inch from the jack. Harry viewed things differently. Countering Bert's proverb with a cry of 'nothing venture, nothing gain,' he slowly approached the launching circle, took aim at Mavis's *boule* and let fly with all the force he could muster.

Harry's aim was immaculate. As Mavis's *boule* was sent speeding off to join Betty's in the long grass, he raised his arms in triumph. But not for long. To his horrow, he saw his own *boule* cannon onto Bert's which then sent the jack to a position midway between the first two *boules* of Betty and Mavis.

'You've blown it,' cried Bert. 'Why didn't you leave well alone like me?'

'Talk about Sod's Law,' muttered Harry. 'I make a brilliant throw and it ends up losing us the match. There's no such thing as justice.'

When Monique wanted to know the meaning of Sod's Law, Mavis explained it was a term used to describe a particularly unlucky, usually ironic, sequence of events. Just when things are going well, fate intervenes and spoils everything. Monique nodded but who was Sod?, she asked. Mavis didn't think Sod was a real person: the name probably came from the colloquial expression 'poor sod,' to describe someone afflicted by a cruel blow of fate.

'So I can tell Harry he is a poor sod?' asked Monique.

'I don't think he'd be too pleased if you did.' replied Mavis smiling. 'It's not very flattering. Just tell him he was very unlucky.'

As they followed Harry and Bert to the bar, Monique had another question for Mavis.

'I didn't know Harry kept chickens. You told him not to count them, Why should he want to count them?'

'I can't imagine Harry keeping chickens,' laughed Mavis. 'We have a proverb 'Don't count your chickems before they're hatched.' When Harry said they would win easily, I wanted to tell him that his prediction was premature. He was being too optimistic assuming all eggs hatch into chickens.'

'We have a proverb meaning exactly the same,' cried Monique. '*Il ne faut pas vendre la peau de l'ours avant de l'avoir tué.* That's just what Harry did! I'll tell him.'

When Harry had bought drinks all round – the least he could do, according to Bert – Monique consoled him by saying how very unlucky he had been. But, she added, he should not have sold the bear's skin before he'd killed it.

'Harry would run a mile if he ever saw a bear, let alone kill it,' commented Bert who tended to take things literally. It was left to Mavis to clarify matters by quoting the proverb in French followed by its English equivalent.

'Those first two lobs of Bert would have made anyone count their chickens,' protested Harry. 'How was I to know they were just a flash in the pan? He never got near the jack after that until he started bowling underarm. And then it was too late.'

'It wouldn't have been too late if you'd played safe with your last *boule*,' retorted Bert. 'You wanted to finish in a blaze of glory, didn't you.'

'You've got to admit, Bert, that my last *boule* was a masterpiece of precision. If Sod hadn't intervened, we'd now be celebrating a glorious victory, as Napoleon no doubt said after Waterloo. Anyway, let's face it, Bert, the ladies deserved to win. If they play as well in the final against Bill and Syd, I think they'll have an easy victory.'

'There you go again, Harry, counting your chickens,' cried Mavis. 'I'd just say we're cautiously optimistic.'

The arrival of Mike, Joe and O.L. put a stop to any further discussion about *boules*.

With only quarter of an hour to go before the meal, Mike and Joe decided to shower later and accept the drinks offered by Harry. They had walked non-stop down the stony track at a brisk pace, resisted the temptation to cut across the countless zigzags and couldn't wait to get their boots off. Olive had had no problem keeping up with them. She had talked about coming back next year to do the *Tour du Mont-Blanc* and asked if they would like to join her.

When she.appeared at table relaxed and smiling, Harry was impressed.

'You look as if you've just been for a stroll round the park, Olive.'

'Well, it was hardly a stroll round the park, Harry, but I must say I feel fine,' she replied. 'Do you realise that the descent from *Index* is 1500 metres! That's like coming down twice from Scafell Pike to Borrowdale!'

Harry felt obliged to point out that he didn't think Mr Wainwright would have used the chair-lift to get up to *Index* in the first place but O.L. ignored this remark and went on to thank Monique for another memorable walk. Would it be possible to show her photos of chamois and marmots to the group after dinner on Monique's computer?

'Just what we had in mind,' interjected Harry. 'I think Monique and I will be able to add some of yours to ours, *n'est-ce pas*, Monique? They'd need editing, of course. If we showed them all, we'd be up till midnight.'

After dinner, Harry included O.L.'s chamois photos and her shots of Mike and Joe scrambling over rocks on the Index path but rejected the rest as technically and artistically inferior to his own close-ups of flowers and his long-range mountain shots.. While these were much admired, it was the human interest photos that were met with most enthusiasm – Mike, Joe and O.L. in the chair-lift, Monique in the lake and Joyce descending the ladder. Less unanimous was the applause for Monique's picture of Harry in blue shorts and floral shirt when Syd and Bill covered their eyes and Bert groaned, saying he'd seen enough of that for one day and didn't want reminding of it.

L'AIGUILLE DU MIDI

'You must be joking!' exploded Bert. 'Me paying 42.50€ for the *Aiguille du Midi*? That's about £35! Not on your life! My wife would think I'd gone mad.'

During breakfast, Harry had asked Bert if he'd changed his mind about taking the cable-car up to the *Aiguille du Midi*. At 3842 metres, they'd be well above the snow line and the panoramic views would be superb. It would be the highlight of their visit.

'And you don't have to stop there,' Mavis had added. 'You can take the gondola across the *Glacier du Géant* to Helbronner in Italy. I did it last year with Monique; it was a marvellous experience.'

'I dare say it was,' replied Bert, 'but it's not for me. I've something else in mind.'

'Not going to hire a mountain bike, are you?' asked Penny.

'That I'd love to see,' added Joyce, 'but I think he'd prefer a mule.'

Harry dismissed both these possibilities on the grounds of cost. In his opinion, Bert was probably planning an all day siesta punctuated by visits to a nearby café.

'Wrong on all counts,' replied Bert. 'I'm going to make a voyage of discovery. I'm going to explore the Chamonix Valley from top to bottom by train and bus.

Monique's given me the timetables and I've got it all planned. I'm taking the 08.55 to Vallorcine. Might have a stroll up the road into Switzerland if I feel like it. On the way back, I'll probably drop off at Argentière for a look round, then I'll catch a bus at 11.52 down to Les Houches. I'll picnic there and get the bus back to Chamonix at 13.30.'

Harry could hardly believe his ears. Bert was usually content to follow where others led. Planning a solo expedition like this was completely out of character, all the more so in a foreign country where he could hardly speak a word of the language! Harry was about to congratulate him when the explanation occurred to him.

'And it won't cost you a penny!' he exclaimed. 'It's all because of the free pass we get for trains and buses in the Chamonix Valley, isn't it? Well, I must say you're running true to form Bert. Never been known to turn down a freebie.'

'Sounds a good idea to me,' said Mike. 'Joe and I are meeting Monique's brother at the heliport this afternoon but we've nothing planned for this morning. Fancy some company, Bert? Just in case you get lost.'

Bert said he'd be pleased to have some company and in reply to Harry's inquiry about his plans for the afternoon, announced that he'd thought about looking round the *Musée Alpin* followed by a swim at the Sports Centre.

'Suppose we meet at the swimming pool at 3 o'clock,' suggested Mavis. 'Monique's mum has invited us to lunch so we won't be going with you to the *Aiguille du Midi*. The queue shouldn't be too long but be prepared for sub-zero temperatures at the top. If you're all going across the glacier, you could picnic at Helbronner.'

There were some hesitation when Monique added that the cost of the cable-car to the *Aiguille* plus the gondola to Helbronner amounted to 66.50€ but in the end, when Mavis said that it was a 'once in a lifetime' experience, all seven decided to go ahead.

As Bert left, accompanied by Mike and Joe, Harry wished him *bon voyage* and told him to use the word *piscine* when he got lost in Chamonix and had to ask for directions. In reply, Bert hoped that Harry wouldn't suffer from altitude sickness at nearly 4000 metres.

At the *Midi* cable-car station, a queue thirty metres long was snaking its way towards the ticket office. Resigning themselves to a lengthy wait, they joined the queue and shuffled slowly forward but it didn't take Harry long to realise the photogenic possibilities round about and he disappeared, camera in hand. What first caught his eye was the electronic sign giving the temperature at the top as -5°. He followed this up by snapping a group of shivering, flimsily dressed tourists who had just come down, a small boy eating a *baguette* as long as his arm and an African family in brightly coloured flowing robes. When he returned to re-join the others, by now almost at the ticket office, he was met by a withering look from O.L.

After changing cable cars at the half-way stage, Penny began to feel ill. The second leg was much steeper than the first and she would have turned back if she hadn't felt trapped in the queue. Encouraged by Betty and Joyce and supported by Bill and Harry, she stumbled into the cable car, propped herself against a window, murmured apologies for being such a nuisance and gratefully accepted O.L.'s offer of smelling salts.

The swaying motion of the car as it docked at the summit ten minutes later, made her feel nauseous but the blast of cold air as she stepped out onto solid ground brought a smile of relief to her face. On the viewing platform, no time was wasted putting on anoraks, hats and gloves but it was the magnifcent mountain scenery all around rather than the cold which took their breath away. O.L. was in her seventh heaven.

'I can't believe we're so near to *Mont-Blanc*,' she cried, pointing to the snow-capped dome with a wisp of cloud above it. I'd guess it's no more than two kilometres as the crow flies. Look, there's a party of climbers down below crossing the glacier. Judging from the orientation table, I think they'll be heading for the *Mont Maudit*.'

Harry left O.L. in full flow to walk all the way round before deciding what photos to take and from where. The visibility was perfect and in addition to the relatively close *Mont-Blanc* chain, there were stunning views across the *Vallée Blanche* of the *Grandes Jorasses* and further away of the Matterhorn in the Swiss Alps. Catching sight of the lift going up to the Pinnacle, he thought about taking his photos from there and went back to find the others clustered round the orientation table with O.L. still pointing out landmarks.

'We're not at the top yet,' he cried. 'There's another 42 metres to get to the Pinnacle. Could be the best place for photos. Don't worry, Penny, there's a lift.'

'I've done enough climbing for one day, thank you very much,' replied Penny. 'When you come down, you'll find Joyce and me in the cafeteria.'

When Betty and Syd opted to join them for coffee, Harry, O.L. and Bill took the lift up to the highest point at 3842 metres. Harry was not disappointed. The unimpeded 360 panorama was all he had hoped for. With his camera in video mode, he circled the viewing platform to capture the full picture, a picture that he thought would have members of his Camera Club sitting on the edge of their seats. Knowing that he would have to add a commentary later, he paid more heed than usual to O.L. as she consulted her map and reeled off the names of the peaks, mountain ranges and glaciers he was filming.

'Not a bad place to have lunch either,' commented Bill, pausing to glance at the menu outside the restaurant aptly named '*Le 3842.*' 'Except that it costs an arm and a leg.'

'I'll book a table for the club when I win the lottery,' promised Harry but O.L. said she'd be happier outside with a cheese sandwich; she'd prefer to feast on the views.

Rejoining the others in the cafeteria, they found Joyce and Penny in high spirits, refreshed by coffee and pleased with the souvenirs and postcards they'd bought. They would write the cards when they got to Helbronner and post them, using the special *Aiguille du Midi* stamp, in the letter box before going down. Hearing how impressed Betty and Syd had been by an exhibition about the construction of the station, O.L. rushed off to find it, leaving Harry and Bill to enjoy their coffee in peace.

Penny found the gondola to Helbronner much less intimidating than the cable car from the *Plan de l'Aiguille*. Once installed, sandwiched between Syd and Bill, she felt safe and began to relax. Harry filmed them all clambering aboard the continuously moving, six-seater egg before it lifted off into space. Last in was Joyce who had forgotten to take off her rucksack and got herself wedged in the doorway. Frantically trying to free herself, she lost her balance and finished up on Syd's lap. Harry got a close-up of the scene just before the doors closed and fell about laughing for so long that he only just managed to climb into the gondola behind where he found himself in the presence of a Spanish couple, a gentleman from Croatia and two Italian students.

On discovering the intruder's nationality, all of them were eager to practise their English and Harry was only too willing to oblige: he couldn't have wished for a more captive audience than this. With occasional pauses to enthuse about and photograph the grandiose scenery, he explained at length what had led up to Thurston Ramblers' visit to Chamonix and gave a graphic account of the walks they'd done.

It was by no means a monologue. Harry discovered that the Italian students had spent a holiday in London, the Spanish couple had walked the West Highland Way and the Croatian gentleman had a daughter who'd married a Welshman and was living in Cardiff. By the time they reached the *Pointe Helbronner* after 45 minutes in the gondola, addresses had been exchanged and Harry had been invited to call on his newly acquired friends whenever he happened to visit Italy, Spain or Croatia.

There was no need for anoraks and gloves when they disembarked. 380 metres lower than the *Midi*, *Helbronner* was a sun-trap and people were either picknicking in shirt-sleeves or sunbathing on the spacious south-facing terrace. Bill warned Joyce and Penny not to expose too much bare flesh and advised everyone to wear sunglasses to protect against the glare of reflected light from the glacier below and the snow higher up.

To Harry, the sharpness of the light was a bonus. Leaving the others to picnic, he walked round, taking photos in all directions. Seen from the Italian side, Mont-Blanc, with its steep rock faces and jagged arêtes, presented a much more formidable challenge than the snowy dome seen from Chamonix. Close at hand to the east towered the *Dent du Géant* at 4013 metres; to the west the *refuge Torino* could be picked out and far below to the south lay the town of Courmayeur.

O.L. had identified landmarks from the *Aiguille du Midi* but this time Harry got in first. Hurriedly finishing her picnic, she went off, map in one hand, binoculars in the other, to verify his sightings.

'I wonder what Bert's doing just now,' mused Joyce.

'Nothing energetic, you can be sure of that,' answered Harry. 'He's probably having a siesta in the train right now: goodness knows where he'll end up.'

'At least he won't get sunburnt in the train,' said Penny. 'I'm roasting here. How about having our siesta in the gondola on the way back?'

'That's all very well,' chimed in Bill, 'but we wouldn't get much sleep if somebody started snoring, would we? In such a confined space, the noise would be deafening.'

Syd took the hint. He didn't feel drowsy but in case he did nod off, he'd let the others take the first gondola and he would take the next one. Harry said that was good news for them but bad news for whoever came next. What Syd needed was a warning notice he could stick on the window, something similar to 'Beware of the Dog.' Like that, he'd have the whole cabin to himself.

In the event, no warning notice was needed. When no-one else joined him, Syd stretched out, made himself comfortable and was soon fast asleep. Looking round, Bill noticed that the gondola behind had acquired an unusual swaying motion.

Back at the *Aiguille du Midi*, Harry treated Syd to a beer as a thank-you for his undisturbed nap. Joyce and Penny posted their cards before joining O.L, Betty and Bill to watch a group of skiers begin their descent of the *Vallée Blanche*. Seeing the steep, slippery slope down to the glacier was enough for Joyce.

'I'd sooner go up in a chair-lift than walk on skis down there,' she exclaimed. 'And then skiing all the way back down to Chamonix, dodging all those crevasses we saw from the gondola! It doesn't bear thinking about.'

'Rubbish!' retorted O.L. 'If you'd been born here, you'd have taken to skis like ducks to water. I only wish I'd had the chance to learn to ski when I was a girl. It must be a wonderful experience, gliding through the snow like those people over there.'

'Too late now for us, Olive,' responded Penny. 'Anyway, I'm freezing, let's get back to Harry and Syd. I hope I don't throw a wobbly on the way down.'

Penny didn't exactly enjoy the descent but she managed to control her vertigo and breathed a sigh of relief on getting back to Chamonix. With half an hour before the rendez-vous with Mavis, Monique and Bert at the pool, O.L announced that she preferred to visit the *Musée Alpin*, after which she would walk the two kilometres along the river back to the hotel.

To their surprise, Bert had got there before them. Standing by the ticket office, he was studying a plan of the sports complex.

'The paddling pool's over there, Harry,' he called out. 'I think it'll be warm enough for you but you'll have to get changed first; you can't just roll your trouser legs up.'

Harry's aversion to cold water was well known. He often swam in the heated indoor pool at home but he'd never been known to swim outdoors. With the sun shining and an air temperature of 26°, it was certainly warm enough outside for him to test the water.

Harry changed into trunks, dipped a foot in the pool and was just debating whether to take the plunge when Bert, creeping up behind him, speeded things up by giving him a push. When Harry surfaced, spluttering and vowing revenge, Bert was so amused that he was unaware of Joyce bearing down on him. Propelled forward by her shove, he almost landed on top of Harry who was none too pleased to be immersed a second time. Rejecting Bert's challenge to a race over a length of the 50 metre pool, he contented himself with floating on his back, enjoying the views of the snow-capped *Mont-Blanc massif*.

The arrival of Mavis and Monique put an end to Harry's contemplation and galvanised him into action. Monique had found a ball which she threw mid way between himself and Bert. Bert got there first but Harry. seeing a chance for revenge, dived down, grabbed his foot and pulled him under. After more splashing about with the ball, all four made several trips down the 17 metre slide followed by a spell under the water jets before joining the others, reclining on *chaises longues*.

Joyce chose this moment to ask Bert if he'd enjoyed his day and had he missed them.

'Yes to question one and no to question two,' replied Bert.

'Well I hope you remembered the Swiss chocolate I asked you to get me,' said Joyce.

'I remembered all right,' answered Bert. 'but there was a little snag when we got to the frontier post. We'd forgotten our passports and they wouldn't let us in.'

'So you drowned your sorrows in the station bar, am I right?' asked Penny.

'Correct,' replied Bert. 'I must say that air-conditioned train was very comfortable.'

'In other words, you fell asleep,' cried Harry.

'As a matter of fact, I did have a little nap after Mike and Joe got out. That's how I met Linda and Carole. They gave me a nudge when we got to *Les Houches*.'

Interrogated by Harry, Bert revealed that he had spent a very pleasant hour in a bar with his newly found companions. They had come from Manchester and were starting the first leg of the *Tour du Mont-Blanc*. After they'd left, he had bought a ham sandwich and a peach, found a shady tree and must have dozed off. When he got back to Chamonix on the bus, there wasn't time to visit the museum so he'd gone straight to the Sports Centre.

'You said you were going on a discovery trip,' exclaimed Harry, 'but all you've done is booze, sleep and chat up girls! You could have done that at home! And what are you going to do with all those euros you haven't spent? How about treating us all to afternoon tea in exchange for the privilege of seeing our brilliant photos? What do you think, ladies?'

Joyce thought it an excellent idea. It would make up for her missing chocolate.

'If we walk back through the woods,' said Monique, 'there's a lovely café where we could have tea on the terrace. But we can't let Bert pay for all nine of us. Suppose Mavis and I each paid a third ... for the privilege of seeing your brilliant photos.'

Bert could hardly reject Monique's offer. If the cost of today's excursion had left Harry destitute, providing him with tea in his hour of need was the least he could do. All the same, he made clear that no more than one bilberry tart was on offer.

During tea on the terrace, Harry's photos were highly acclaimed by Monique and Mavis. Bert was rather less enthusiastic. The names of the mountains added by Harry meant nothing to him and after ten minutes' viewing, he couldn't suppress a yawn. Just as he was nodding off, a peel of laughter from Mavis made him jump awake.

'Look at this. Bert!' she cried, 'Joyce on Syd's lap getting into the gondola. I don't know which of them looks more startled.'

'I'd say Syd.' replied Bert. 'He looks shell-shocked. After all, he's not as well cushioned as Joyce. Personally, I'd sooner collapse on Joyce than have her collapse on me.'

'Cheeky monkey.' retorted Joyce. 'You're all skin and bone. If you fell on top of me, I'd be full of cuts and bruises.'

On the walk back to the hotel, Harry proposed to show his photos after dinner on the television screen: enlarged, they would be much sharper and more impressive. Mike and Joe would certainly be interested as, no doubt, would O.L. Bert too was welcome to join them if he could manage to stay awake.

'What about the *boules* final?' asked Bill. 'Fancy playing before dinner, Mavis and Betty? Syd and I are up for it if you can adjudicate, Monique. Admission free for well-behaved spectators.'

With Penny and Joyce cheering on Mavis and Betty, Harry and Bert felt obliged to support Bill and Syd. It was not a match for purists. Several guests came along but kept a safe distance from the *piste* as *boules* flew in all directions. When Syd's deliveries were spectacularly erratic, Bert suggested the match be postponed on the grounds that Syd had not had enough time to recover from being squashed by Joyce.

'Rubbish,' retorted Joyce. 'Syd was no better when he played against us. You're just trying to find an excuse for losing.'

When the sun disappeared briefly behind a cloud, Bill, at Harry's instigation, appealed against the light but Monique would have none of it. With the score at 10 – 4 in favour of the ladies, Mavis said that the only way to salvage male pride was for Harry to get down on his knees and pray for rain. In the end, Bill and Syd magnanimously conceded defeat and congratulated Mavis and Betty on their consistency. Harry, in a last ditch attempt to save the day, appeared less chivalrous.

'How is it,' he announced, 'that you and Betty never played as well as that against Bert and me? You only won by a fluke! I maintain that your enhanced performance today can only be accounted for by the consumption of illegal substances. Until this matter is resolved, I consider the result of the match null and void.'

Harry's little joke was wasted on Joyce. Taking him seriously, she bluntly told him to get lost. He was nothing but a male chauvinist pig. Women had once again demonstrated their ability to compete with men on equal terms and it was high time he accepted the fact. On the way to the bar, Mavis tried to convince her that Harry was just ... being Harry. It was only when he'd bought drinks all round and proposed a toast to 'The Ladies, God Bless 'Em' that Joyce was prepared to admit she'd overreacted.

As they assembled in the garden for the evening meal, the hotel owner, Monique's uncle Claude, asked if they had had a good day.

'*Magnifique*,' cried O.L. before launching into a list of all the mountains she had seen and photographed. When her French couldn't adequately express her delight, she continued unperturbed in English, unaware that Claude's command of English was no better than her command of French. Claude kept nodding politely: he didn't understand what she was saying but her body language spoke volumes.

'*Je vois que vous aimez bien la montagne, madame,*' he interposed before excusing himself and rushing back to the kitchen.

At table, O.L. told Monique what a charming man her uncle was.

'Oh yes,' replied Monique, 'he is very popular with the ladies, just like your 'Arrry.'

O.L. spluttered over her soup at this but refrained from comment, leaving Monique free to ask Mike and Joe about their guided visit of the Mountain Rescue Base.

'It was great,' said Mike, 'we really enjoyed it. *Henri* showed us all the equipment they use and the protective clothing they wear when they're called out. He told us how they tried to locate people buried in avalanches, and how they dealt with climbing accidents and lost walkers.'

'What I liked most,' added Joe, 'was getting inside the helicopter. *Henri* showed us the controls and explained how everything worked. Fascinating. While we were in the control room, a call came in from a climber who'd fallen and broken a leg. Within minutes, a helicopter was airborne, guided by radio control to the scene of the accident. We were very impressed by their speed of reaction.'

'Unlike Joyce getting into the gondola,' chipped in Bert. 'She nearly got stuck in the door. Frightened the life out of Syd when she landed on top of him. Wait till you see Harry's photo tonight on the TV screen. It's a hoot.'

When Mavis asked if she'd enjoyed her visit to the *Musée Alpin*, O.L.'s eyes lit up. She had been thrilled to read about the first ascent of *Mont-Blanc* in 1786, how *Balmat* and *Paccard* after several failed attempts, reached the summit to claim the reward offered by the wealthy Swiss mountaineer *de Saussure*.

'What about the women who got to the top?' asked

Mavis. 'Did you see what they were wearing? *Henriette d'Angeville* wore pantaloons and a petticoat down to her ankles.'

'And a feathered beret with a black boa round her neck,' added O.L. 'She was an aristocrat; she did the climb with six guides and six porters! And apparently, she opened a bottle of champagne on the top! But that was in 1838 and she wasn't the first woman to reach the summit, although she claimed to be.'

'I bet that would have been you, Olive, if you'd been around then,' called out Harry. 'I can picture you in a feathered beret and a black boa but I can't imagine you taking champagne up. You nearly blew a gasket when I offered wine to Monique in Teesdale last year.'

O.L. didn't think Harry's interruption worthy of reply and went on.

'The first woman to climb *Mont-Blanc* was an eighteen year old peasant girl called *Marie Paradis* – thirty years before *Henriette*. Just imagine, eighteen years old! She said she was 'pulled, pushed and carried' at some stage but she made it in the end. *Henriette* claimed to be the first woman to do the climb unaided but I think she couldn't accept that a mere peasant girl had beaten her to it.'

'When you think of their primitive clothing and gear,' said Mike, 'you realise what an achievement it was.'

'All the more so because they didn't have the luxury of mountain huts to sleep in,' added Joe. ' What's more, there were no cable cars or railway to take them part way up.'

'Or helicopters to rescue them if they got into

trouble,' said Monique. 'Even nowadays there are fatal accidents every year on *Mont-Blanc*.'

'Mention of fatal accidents makes me think of Edward Whymper's disastrous descent of the Matterhorn in 1865,' continued O.L. 'Out of the seven climbers in the party, all roped together, only three survived. One of them fell and dragged three more to their death. It was only because the rope snapped that Whymper and the two others didn't follow them.'

'Do you know Whymper died and was buried here in Chamonix?' asked Mavis. 'His grave is in the Protestant churchyard.'

'I went straight there after leaving the museum,' replied O.L. It's very moving: no marble headstone or pious epitaph, just a jagged peak-shaped rock with a plaque embedded in it. What an adventurous life he led! Apart from his many first ascents in the Alps, he made climbing and scientific expeditions to the Andes, Greenland and the Canadian Rockies. He also wrote books and illustrated them.'

'A man after your own heart, Olive,' cried Harry. 'Could it be that your hero Mr Wainwright has been relegated to second place?'

'I admire them both, if that's what you mean. Just like I admire *Marie Paradis*. Serious people with the energy and determination to achieve their goals, come what may.'

'That cuts you out, Harry!' exclaimed Bert. 'You're not serious enough. I don't think you rate very highly on energy and determination either ... except when it's a case of reaching a pub before closing time.'

'Oh come on, Bert, that's hardly fair,' interposed

Mavis. 'You're talking about last year's Harry. You've got to admit that this year's model is a big improvement on the old version. I think he's shown quite a lot of energy and determination since then.'

'O.K., I grant you he's improved but I'm not convinced it'll last.' retorted Bert. 'He's not consistent. He was struggling coming down from *Montenvers*. It wouldn't surprise me if next year's Harry turned out to be like last year's Harry.'

'Thanks for that vote of confidence, Bert old pal. Time wil tell: you'll just have to wait and see. Meanwhile, *messieurs-dames*, if you'll excuse me, this year's Harry will now go and prepare for this evening's photographic extravaganza. Entrance is free but a retiring collection will be made in aid of the Rejuvenate Bert Appeal. This will enable our good friend to spend a week at a health farm. You know the kind of place I mean, one lettuce leaf and a carrot for breakfast washed down with a litre of spring water. Ice-cold baths, steaming saunas, mud packs, body massages, work-outs in the gym, that sort of thing. No greasy fry ups, spicey sausage rolls, cream cakes or sweet tea. Total ban on alcohol of course. With a bit of luck, a new Bert will emerge, rejuvenated, at the end of the week.'

Harry was on stage. Holding up a hand to silence the titters from his audience, he continued:

'Now it has to be said, ladies and gentlemen, that sartorially speaking, our good friend Bert leaves a lot to be desired. What remains of your donations will therefore be allocated to remedying this state of affairs. We have already made a start by providing him with a brand new anorak. Let us now finish what we've started. A well-fitting pair of trousers, a brightly coloured shirt or two, some shiny new boots and a packet of razor blades would all be desirable. Oh, how could I forget, a decent hat to replace his old woolly bonnet. And maybe a monthly season ticket to the barbers, if funds permit. I trust you will give generously, *messieurs-dames*: a worthier cause, I'm sure you will agree, would be hard to find.'

Monique, who didn't fully understand the curious rapport between Harry and Bert, was reliieved to see that Bert was not in the least offended. On the contrary, he seemed to find Harry's performance as amusing as everyone else.

'I must say you're on good form tonight, Harry. You can take it for granted that all contributions will be gratefully received. If anyone's short of euros, I'd be prepared to accept stirling. Perhaps you'd care to visit me at the health farm, Harry? On second thoughts, perhaps not: they might think your need was greater than mine with all the flab you'll have put back on by then.'

When O.L. put a stop to these exchanges by asking curtly if there was still time to view the photos, Harry left, saying the show would begin in five minutes. Bert left soon afterwards: he'd no desire to see any more of Harry's photos, however brilliant they were and would go for a little stroll. On his way back, he bumped into Joyce, Penny and Betty followed by Bill and Syd.

'Couldn't stand Harry droning on any longer,' explained Syd. 'Started nodding off.'

'Nodding off?' cried Bill. 'You were rumbling like an avalanche! I had to drag you out before everyone dived for cover.'

Left with an audience of five, Harry showed all his own photos but when Monique said she'd have to be going home now, Mavis, Mike and Joe followed her out. With only O.L. remaining, Harry looked at his watch.

'Getting a bit late, Olive, don't you think?' Suppose we leave your photos for another time ... when we've a full complement.'

O.L. could only agree. She doubted if Harry had ever intended to show her photos.

LE GLACIER DU TOUR

Bert's appearance for breakfast created a stir. For maximum effect, he had delayed his entrance until all were present. Framed in the doorway wearing sun-glasses and sporting a sky-blue shirt, dark brown shorts, a peaked cap with ear and neck flaps, all brand new, he waited for the reaction.

'It can't be! Yes it is! I'd recognise those nobbly knees anywhere,' exclaimed Harry. 'It's Bert in fancy dress! Pretending to be Lawrence of Arabia.'

'Left your camel in the garden, Bert?' enquired Bill.

'Where did you get that hat, where did you get that hat?' sang Joyce and Penny in unison.

'It's a big improvement on his old one, anyway,' added Harry, 'and I must admit that shirt is rather fetching. Stumble on a car boot sale yesterday, did you Bert?'

'No I did not!' cried Bert, grinning. 'Bought them in a shop – 50% off.'

'Trust you to find a bargain,' said Joyce. 'If you wear your new anorak over that lot, your wife won't recognise you.'

'I think Bert's anorak might be baptised today,' interposed Mike. 'The sun's shining at the moment but there's a lot of cloud about.'

When Monique arrived after breakfast, she

confirmed Mike's opinion: the local weather forecast predicted the possibility of a storm late afternoon so they must not forget to take waterproofs. She hoped everyone was on good form because they would be climbing 790 metres to reach the *Albert Premier refuge* on the *glacier du Tour*.

O.L. beamed at this. She was sure they were all capable of climbing 790 metres if they put their minds to it. It was just a question of will-power. Penny and Joyce exchanged glances with Harry: all three felt targeted by O.L.'s last remark.

'We won't be taking one of those horrible chair-lifts, I hope,' cried Joyce.

'No we won't,' replied Monique. 'We'll take the cable car from the village of *Le Tour* to *Charamillon* and start our walk from there. We could take the chair-lift higher to the *Col de Balme* which would shorten the climb to 522 metres but I think you'll be happier starting from *Charamillon*.'

Joyce and Penny nodded emphatically and when Mavis casually remarked that they would save 10€ by not taking the chair-lift, Bert loudly expressed approval. His spirits were further raised when Mavis added that the bus ride to *Le Tour* would cost them precisely nothing, assuming no-one forgot to bring the Guest Card provided by the hotel.

Inevitably, it was Joyce who couldn't lay hands on her Guest Card. After frantically turning out all her pockets, she rushed up to her room, returning red-faced to say she must have lost it yesterday at the swimming pool.

'Oh really, Joyce,' exclaimed O.L., 'it's time you got yourself organised. You couldn't find your boarding card at the airport and now you're holding us up again. You'll just have to pay on the bus.'

'No, no,' cried Monique, 'I'll go and get another card for Joyce from my uncle. I'll catch you up at the bus stop.'

As the bus climbed the 400 metres to *Le Tour*, O.L. was fascinated by the wooden chalets with their steep roofs, shutters and window-boxes full of geraniums. In answer to her question, Monique explained that the poles lying at intervals across the roofs held back the snow so that it didn't slide down all at once and bury anyone underneath. They served the same purpose as *paravalanches*, screens built on steep slopes above roads and railways to hold back the snow. If a road or railway crossed an avalanche path, a box-like tunnel with a sloping roof would be built to prevent huge build-ups of snow and keep traffic moving.

'We don't have anything like as much snow as you,' said Joe, 'but it only takes an inch or two for everything to grind to a halt.'

'Here we are always happy when the snow comes,' laughed Monique. 'Without it, Chamonix would be a ghost town in the winter. Snow gives employment to so many people in hotels, restaurants, shops and ski schools. We have to keep the roads open to make sure that the *pistes* are accessible. Snow-ploughs work all night long if necessary.'

'I imagine that a lot of people in the valley have 4-wheel drives,' remarked Mike. 'They must be essential for anyone living in remote areas.'

'Yes they are,' answered Monique. 'Alternatively, we change to winter tyres and carry a set of chains. Some people leave their cars at home and go to work on skis or snowshoes. We've learnt to live with snow.'

Living with snow! A wave of nostalgia carried O.L. back to her childhood memories of the big freeze of '47. How exciting it had been, struggling to school through snowdrifts taller than herself! She recalled the sledge she had dragged to the village shop to collect whatever food was available. The power lines were down and her mother had to cook by candle light on an open fire using wood when they ran out of coal.

O.L. had always loved snow. It transformed the world, made beautiful what was nondescript. Its gently falling flakes were hypnotic. It brought people together. All the same, snow had to be kept in its place; like fire it was a good servant but a bad master. To O.L., snow was not just a thing of beauty, it was also a challenge. Man against nature. Her heroes were men and women who had defied the elements. She had already made up her mind to return to Chamonix in the summer to walk round *Mont-Blanc* but now, the more she thought about a winter visit, the more attractive it became. Walking on snowshoes would be no problem and she would learn to ski on the dry ski slope near home. It would be an adventure, a challenge. People like Harry Birch would no doubt say she was too old for skiing. She would prove them wrong. There was still time for her to learn how to live with snow.

'You O.K., Olive?' asked Mavis as they got off the bus at *Le Tour*. 'You seem a bit preoccupied.'

'Just trying to imagine what it's like living up here when the snow comes,' replied O.L. 'It must be magical.'

Mavis was not so sure. 'I dare say it is if you're young and fit but it can't be much fun for the old and infirm. I bet they get sick of the sight of snow.'

According to Monique there weren't many people who still lived in the village all year round: a lot of the chalets in the vicinity were holiday homes or let in the winter months to families who came to ski. *Le domaine de Balme* was very popular with skiers and snowboarders of all levels: nursery slopes for children and beginners, more demanding runs for experienced skiers and *hors-pistes* for the adventurous. They would see how vast the area was as they went up in the cable car to *Charamillon*.

When Mike asked about the danger of avalanche if skiers and boarders went off-piste, he was told there were no-go zones and prominent signs indicated avalanche risk on a scale of 1 to 5. People wanting to ski off-piste should always take a guide and be equipped with DVA – *Détecteur de Victimes d'Avalanche*- an electronic device that transmitted and received signals, formerly called *ARVA*.

'Your brother demonstrated one to us yesterday,' cried Joe. 'He blindfolded us, hid the 'victim's' DVA somewhere outside and we had to locate it. When our DVA picked up a bleep, we paced up and down guided by the strength of the signal.'

Betty wanted to know how long it took to find the 'victim.'

'About three or four minutes but we were only searching a small space,' replied Joe.

'After an avalanche, victims can be buried over a very wide area and finding them could take much longer. It's a race against time. *Henri* told us that their chances of survival decrease rapidly after fifteen minutes.'

'So your DVA is bleeping loud and clear, what happens next?' asked Bill.

'Rescuers use long poles to probe through the snow,' went on Mike, 'trying to locate the victim's exact position and find out how deeply they are buried. Then it's a case of digging them out as quickly as possible with the folding spade that guides always carry in their rucksacks.'

'Sounds awful,' exclaimed Joyce. 'I saw a film on TV last year of an avalanche: the devastation it caused was horrendous. Trees snapped like matchsticks and chalets were swept away in a matter of seconds. And it wasn't only snow that did the damage; there were rocks and all sorts of debris mixed up in it as well. How anyone could survive something like that, I can't imagine.'

'It was just like that at Monroc in 1999,' said Monique. 'I was fourteen then and I remember vividly the photos in the local paper and all the controversy that followed. Twelve people died in that avalanche and fourteen buildings were completely destroyed. The snow came down the mountain with such force that it crossed the river *Arve*, climbed up the other side of the valley and engulfed the hamlet of Monroc, only a few kilometres from where we are now. What made it so difficult to accept was that Monroc had been classified as a no risk zone although there had been avalanches there before in 1970 and 1978. In the court case that followed, the mayor of Chamonix was found guilty of second degree murder and given a suspended sentence of three months imprisonment.'

'Sounds like rough justice to me,' commented Bill. 'How could they pin the blame on him for a natural disaster?'

'They thought he had ignored warnings from local people that an avalanche was imminent and should have ordered the hamlet to be evacuated,' replied Monique.

After these grim revelations, there was little talk in the cable-car going up to *Charamillon* but spirits rose when they stepped out and looked at the skyline above and the valley below. Near neighbours *Les* Drus, 3754 metres and *La Verte,* 4122 metres were sharply outlined. Beyond them were the jagged peaks of the *Aiguilles de Chamonix* and the *Aiguille du Midi.* In the distance, stood *Mont-Blanc,* 4807 metres, its white dome topped by a wisp of cloud.

'I'd like a group photo before we start,' called Harry, 'with the mountains in the background. I think I'll get the best angle from the chalet-restaurant higher up.'

'Good idea, Harry.' cried Bert. 'While you're messing about deciding where you want us, we'll have time for coffee. All agreed? Oh and another thing, don't put me in the back row behind Joyce like you usually do. My new outfit deserves maximum exposure.'

O.L. met Bert's proposal to have coffee with a snort. They would be wasting enough time as it was over the photo without wasting more over coffee. By the time Harry had decided on the ideal spot, arranged the group to his and Bert's satisfaction, waited for a passing cloud to reveal the sun and found a waiter to take the photo, O.L.'s patience had reached breaking point.

'No time for dawdling now,' she cried, looking pointedly in the direction of Penny, Joyce and Harry. 'It'll probably take us three hours to get up to the refuge and two hours to get down. Don't forget that the last cable-car leaves at 5 o'clock. Unless you want to walk back down to *Le Tour*, we'd better get moving. No more stopping for photos.'

'She's doing it again,' said Harry to Mavis and Monique as O.L. strode on, twenty yards ahead. 'Taking over from the leader and being bossy. I was hoping she might mellow with age but I should have known better. The leopard cannot change its spots.'

'Oh come on, Harry,' retorted Mavis, 'you did take an age with that photo! O.L. wasn't the only one to get impatient. We were all getting a bit fed up.'

'''Arry 'as taught me another proverb,' cried Monique, 'and this time I can guess what it means. We say *chasser le naturel, il revient au galop.*'

Harry burst out laughing when Mavis gave him the literal translation.

'That's just right for O.L. She's always got to be galloping. I suppose it's second nature to her. I bet she led her mother a dance when she was a kid. Anyway, she's not going to change now, that's for sure. Here's another proverb for you, Monique, 'What can't be cured must be endured.' We just have to put up with her as she is.'

'*Il faut savoir accepter l'inévitable*,' replied Monique promptly. '*C'est ça, n'est-ce pas?*'

The path climbed steadily round the edge of a vast coomb to meet the track coming down from the *Col de Balme* on the Swiss border. O.L. by this time was nowhere to be seen but Monique called for a pause. Joyce and Penny had kept up well. With the sun making only sporadic appearances, they had found the heat less oppressive but were still glad to get their feet up. Mike was less happy with the change in the weather. There was now more white cloud than blue sky. He recalled the cloudburst which had forced Joe and himself to abort their climb to the *Aiguille du Moine* and how relieved they had been to get back safely to the hotel at M*ontenvers*. It was not an experience he'd like to repeat, especially with a group of twelve people mostly new to walking in alpine terrain.

It was during the pause that they were overtaken by three young men, obviously climbers, who recognised Monique. After the customary kissing on both cheeks, all four were soon engaged in animated conversation punctuated by outbursts of laughter. Harry, standing nearby, could make nothing of what they were talking about but it was clear from their body language that all three were on very friendly terms with Monique. When introduced, Harry shook their hands claiming to be *enchanté* but was so bewildered by their questions that he apologised for his poor French, wished them *bonne journée* and withdrew in relief to join Bert and Mavis.

'Been weighing up the opposition, have you Harry?' grinned Bert. 'I must say I don't rate your chances. You're a bit too long in the tooth for a young lass like Monique. I'm surprised she's still unattached. Those three lads obviously fancy her.'

'They're not the only ones,' added Mavis. 'She has a whole string of admirers. I've met some of them. Sporty types, mostly. They all go skiing and climbing together.'

Harry concealed his dismay as best he could. On his first meeting with Monique a year ago in Teesdale, he had been attracted by her good looks and sense of humour. It was mainly to see her again that he had agreed to come to Chamonix. He had attended evening classes to improve his French and had hired a personal trainer to lose weight and get fit.

Now he was forced to accept the fact that whatever he did to impress Monique, there was no way of bridging the generation gap between them.

'They're old school friends of mine,' announced Monique after they had left. 'They're spending the night in the refuge and climbing *l'Aiguille du Tour* tomorow. They're planning to climb in the Himalayas next year and asked if I'd like to join them. I'd love to but the dates don't fall in my school holidays.'

'Can't see Harry climbing in the Himalayas,' said Bert sotto voce to Mavis. 'Not even the new Harry. Can you?'

'Frankly, no,' replied Mavis. 'That would be asking too much.'

It was not until they arrived at a rocky section of the path equipped with handrails that they met up with O.L. coming back towards them.

'You've been so long, I was beginning to think you'd had an accident,' she shouted. 'Anyway, I've been up and down this ledge and there's nothing to worry about. Just hang on to the rail and mind where you're putting your feet.'

Following Mike, Joyce and Penny gingerly made their way down.

'Don't tiptoe!' yelled O.L. 'You're not walking on

thin ice. You want as much contact wiith the ground as possible. Plant your feet firmly on the stones!'

Joyce did as she was told and made quicker progress but slipped when almost on level ground. Luckily, she fell into Mike's outstretched arms and both managed to stay on their feet.

'Nice one, Joyce,' called Bert. 'Can we have a replay for the camera? I'll take Mike's place, if you like, while he's getting his breath back.'

'You won't,' retorted Joyce. 'I've got my reputation to think about.'

As they climbed steadily round the steep, boulder-strewn hillside, the glacier came into view on their right, causing a buzz of excitement. Reaching the moraine, they re-grouped to survey the scene. Below and in front of them was a wide expanse of stones and rocks beyond which rose a jumble of huge, wierdly shaped, grey/black blocks of ice brought into relief by occasional patches of snow. Higher up, on the skyline, behind a jagged line of seracs could be seen the summit of the *Aiguille du Chardonnet* at 3824 metres.

'Not a pretty sight, really,' commented Mike. 'I suppose this glacier is shrinking like all the others. I imagine it once went all the way down to *Le Tour*. It must have been worrying for people living there.'

'The glacier has certainly retreated a long way since then,' said Monique, 'but there was a disaster here in 1949. Huge walls of ice broke away lower down and killed six people'.

Mavis found it hard to imagine how glaciers could be continually moving.

'When the snow begins to melt,' explained Monique, 'streams underneath the ice act as a lubricant. If you think about the weight of all that ice lying on the gradient, it's easier to understand. Where the pressure builds up, the ice cracks and forms crevasses. We'll see some when we walk up the moraine.'

'Gird your loins for the last lap, Penny,' called Harry. 'Only another 200 metres to climb. You can see the refuge perched on that rocky spur up there.'

'Oh for the wings of a dove,' murmured Penny grimly. 'The spirit is willing but the legs are weak. We'll get there, Joyce and I, but it may take a while. Don't wait for us.'

Running alongside the glacier, the path became rockier and increasingly steep, culminating in a series of zigzags leading up to the refuge. First to arrive was O.L. Standing on the terrace, she took a photo of the others, now well spread out, as they toiled up over the rocks towards her. By the time Penny and Joyce arrived, twenty minutes later, she had followed a path above the refuge leading to a spectacular viewpoint over the glacier.

'I've found the perfect spot to picnic,' she exclaimed. 'The views all round are superb – seracs and crevasses on the glacier, *le Chardonnet* beyond and the *Aiguille du Tour* behind. You can see the *Aiguilles Rouges* on the other side of the valley.'

O.L.'s enthusiasm fell on deaf ears. Slumped at a table on the terrace, Penny and Joyce were clearly exhausted; Betty and Mavis were stretched out on benches and Bert was already delving into his rucksack for food.

'First things first, Olive,' cried Harry. 'That view

will still be there when we've had something to eat and drink here on the terrace. Bert's just about to offer me a beer if he can make it as far as the bar, right Bert?'

'Wrong, Harry,' retorted Bert. 'For the moment, I'm quite happy with tap water. I might buy you a beer later ... to go with the bilberry tart you're just about to offer me.'

Food was forgotten when a blustery wind and a sharp drop in temperature caused everyone to cover up rapidly. Angry looking black clouds were swirling round the tops and it was clear that the rain, anticipated by Mike, would soon be with them.

The first drops were falling as they re-packed picnics and rushed into the refuge.

'What's the hurry Bert?' called Harry. 'Now's just the time to try out your new anorak and you're running inside! Afraid it might get wet, are you? Anyway, you can take it off now unless you're waiting for me to take your photo.'

With the rain lashing against the windows and bouncing on the tables outside, Betty expressed what everyone was feeling.

'Haven't we been lucky, getting here in time. There was nowhere to shelter on our way up, was there. We'd have been soaked.'

A vivid flash of lightning followed two seconds later by a loud clap of thunder made them feel even more relieved to be under cover.

'That's what bothers me more than the rain,' said Mike, 'being caught by a thunderstorm out in the open where there's no place to hide.'

'I wouldn't know what to do for the best,' exclaimed

Joyce. 'What would you do, Mike, in a case like that?'

O.L. didn't give Mike time to reply.

'I'll tell you what you don't do!' she cried. 'Shelter under a tree or a boulder. And to continue walking is just as bad, if not worse.'

Mike agreed; to reduce the risk of being struck by lightning, you should make yourself as small as possible and literally sit it out. Not an easy thing to do, he added, as your instinctive reaction is to find shelter. Of course, if you're walking with a metal stick or poles, you lay them down on the ground some distance from where you're sitting.

Harry left the room to stand at the open door, camera in hand. The chance of a photo of forked lightning against a background of black cloud and mountain peaks was not to be missed. Dramatic shots like this would certainly be much admired by members of his camera club back home.

The storm showed no signs of abating when Mike joined him.

'Better then a fireworks display, this,' cried Harry as flashes of lightning continued to streak across the sky. 'I've got some brilliant photos.'

'I grant you it looks impressive from here,' replied Mike, 'but what concerns me is getting back down to the valley. Much more of this torrential rain and the paths will be awash. At best, they'll be very slippery and at worst, they could be blocked by landslides.'

Monique noticed the worried expression on Mike's face when they rejoined the group.

'I don't think the storm will last long,' she reassured

him, 'but it might take us longer than I imagined to get back to *Charamillon*. I think we should leave here no later than half past two. That should give us plenty of time to catch the last cable car at five o'clock.'

'I wouldn't mind spending the night here,' announced Bert. 'there are some very good smells coming from the kitchen and I see they even have draught beer.'

O.L. was also impressed by the refuge though not for the same reasons. She felt at ease in an environment like this. It pleased her to see groups of walkers and climbers eating together, laughing, joking or in animated conversation, unperturbed by the weather outside. She felt they had something in common. After making a tour of inspection with Mavis of the dormitories, washrooms, showers, toilets and locker rooms, she declared that the refuge had surpassed her expectations: it was indeed more like a hotel.

'As long as you don't mind two-tier beds and no en-suite facilties,' laughed Mavis.

'Actually, it's the biggest and most popular refuge in the area with beds for 140 people. It was built more than fifty years ago and called *Albert Premier* in memory of the Belgian king who did a lot of climbing hereabouts.'

'All this rain's given me a thirst, Bert,' called Harry. 'How about that beer you were going to get me?'

'Sorry mate, no can do. I'm too tightly wedged between Joyce and Penny – and very nice it is too. The only way I could get to the bar would be to crawl under the table but with my fragile back …'

'Come off it,' replied Harry. 'The only thing likely to give you pain is opening your wallet. Anyway, far be it from me to prise you away from the charms of Joyce and Penny. I'll buy the beers and you can return the compliment when we get down to *Le Tour.*'

Making his way to the bar, Harry noticed Monique chatting to the three young climbers they'd met earlier but decided against joining them. He'd be out of his depth in more ways than one. A beer and bilberry tart would provide him with some consolation.

'It's easing off now and the sky's a lot brighter.' called out Mike, coming in from the doorway. 'Looks like you'll not get the chance of spending the night here, after all Bert.'

'Can't say I regret that,' exclaimed Joyce. 'I don't fancy crawling out of one of those bunk beds in the middle of the night to find my way to the loo.'

'Not to mention finding your way back,' added Mavis. 'Who knows where you'd finish up! Next to Bert maybe!'

O.L. put an end to further speculation about where Joyce might end up by announcing her intention of going back up to the viewpoint above the refuge to take photos. She would do this as soon as the rain had stopped; anyone wishing to accompany her would be welcome. Monique looked dubious. It would mean clambering over wet rocks where a slip could have serious consequences, not just for the person who slipped but for the whole group. When no-one volunteered to go with her, Monique felt obliged to exercise her authority as group leader.

'I'd rather you didn't go up there alone, Olive,' she said tactfully. 'I'm sure you'd be very careful but accidents can happen to anyone in conditions like these.'

O.L. hid her frustration as best she could. Shrugging her shoulders, she accepted Monique's advice, knowing that in the circumstances, she could hardly do otherwise.

When the rain had finally stopped, glimpses of sun began to break through the cloud as they assembled on the terrace.

'I said the storm wouldn't last long,' cried Monique. '*Après la pluie, le beau temps!* Do you know that proverb, Arry?'

Harry said he understood the general idea, be optimistic, look on the bright side, things can only get better. He was sure there was something like that in English. It was on the tip of his tongue but he couldn't get it out.

'Every cloud has a silver lining,' called Mavis, coming to his rescue.

'What a lovely expression!' exclaimed Monique. 'I must remember that. It will console me if I fail my English exams next year. Did you know I want to become an English teacher, Arry?'

'No, I didn't,' replied Harry, 'but I'm sure you'll make a very good one. Your English has improved by leaps and bounds since last year. Mind you, you still drop your aitches at times. Say this three times quickly, 'helpful Harry hastily handed her his handkerchief.'

Monique's first attempt met with peels of laughter. Harry then invited everyone to join in. Waving his arms about like a conductor, he increased the tempo and the volume until they were breathless. Spectators emerging from the refuge broke into applause and one of Monique's admirers asked if they were performing an ancient ritual, like a war chant before going into battle.

'Tell him it's an old English custom to celebrate the return of the sun,' said Harry. 'It'll be easier that way.'

On keaving the refuge, no-one needed to be told to proceed with care. Descending the zig-zags on the steep, rocky path, now wet and unstable, took even longer than their slow, laborious ascent a few hours earlier. Mike and Joe led the way. Neither used sticks but apart from a few stumbles, had no major problem. Less sure-footed and much less confidant, the others slowly worked their way down, testing each rock before putting their weight on it.

O.L. had to admit she was glad of the stick she had reluctantly acquired after sliding down Pen-y-Ghent in the snow. Prior to that, she had considered walking sticks to be geriatric, unworthy of serious fell-walkers. Even afterwards, she still disliked using her stick. Strapped on her rucksack, it was for emergency use only. Now, as she probed and slithered from rock to rock, she realised its worth.

Walking down the moraine alongside the glacier was easier but they still had to concentrate on where they were putting their feet and not a word was spoken until they reached the junction where they had stopped to survey the glacier on the way up.

'You can leave your new anorak on, Bert,' called Harry. 'The sun's here to stay so there's no chance of getting it wet. I bet you've got wet feet though; those boots you're wearing look shot at. You're not going to tell me they're waterproof.'

'My boots are waterproof, bulletproof and shockproof,' announced Bert proudly. 'They've clocked up a few thousand miles already and I reckon they're good for another thousand or two. Granted they're a bit scuffed and the sole's a bit thin, but so what?'

Harry demanded to see what he meant by 'a bit thin.'

'A bit thin! There's hardly any tread on them! If there was a boot MOT, they'd have no chance of passing. You'd be breaking the law wearing them!'

'If they're not bust, don't fix 'em, that's my motto,' retorted Bert, carefully folding his anorak to put into his rucksack. 'You won't see me toffed up with the latest flashy gear.'

More on Bert's side than Harry's, O.L. pointed out that no-one could accuse Mr Wainwright of being a flashy dresser and he'd managed very well with a pair of army surplus boots and a tweed jacket. She herself deplored the throw-away society. Anyway, wasn't it time they got moving.

Joyce had not been looking forward to negotiating the rocky section where she'd fallen into the arms of Mike. The stone slabs were now slippery, making her progress painfully slow. Again following Mike, she clung grimly on to the rail and this time managed to stay on her feet, unlike Bert who skidded on a rock and finished up with his legs dangling over the edge.

'It's those boots,' shouted Harry. 'they'll be the death of you one of these days. I'm going to organise a Boots for Bert appeal when we get home. The local paper will lap it up. I can just see the headline, 'Rescue Hero Needs Boots. '

Bert picked himself up and rubbed his back ruefully. He was touched by his old pal's concern for his welfare but there was really no need to go as far as that. He'd actually been toying with the idea of a re-sole for some months. Maybe Harry had a point. Maybe it was now time to take the plunge. He would give the matter further thought.

'Don't leave it until you're on crutches, that's all,' said Harry.

'That would be like shutting the stable door after the horse has bolted, would it not?' asked Monique smiling. 'Have I got it right this time, Harry?'

'Word perfect, Monique. Couldn't have done it better myself. You're a very good pupil. I wish my French was half as good as your English.'

'What do you expect, Harry?' chimed in Bert. 'Can't teach an old dog new tricks, you know. That's another one for your collection, Monique. Know what it means?'

Monique said she thought it meant that old people can't learn to do new things. In French, they would say 'on n'apprend pas à un vieux singe à faire des grimaces' which Mavis translated as 'you can't teach an old monkey to pull faces.'

'Why would anyone want to do that?' asked Penny.

'Maybe organ-grinders,' said Betty. 'They used to have a monkey on a chain to attract an audience and collect the money. A monkey that didn't amuse the crowd wouldn't be good for trade so I imagine the organ-grinder had to teach it to pull faces.'

'And he found that an old monkey, like Harry, wasn't up to it,' added Bert. 'Sorry, Harry, you've left it too late I remember how you used to act the fool in French lessons.'

'That, Bert, I cannot dispute,' replied Harry soberly. 'I was not Ma Sidebottom's star pupil, to be sure. Nor were you, for that matter, I seem to recall. She wasn't a bundle of laughs, old Ma Sidebottom. Now if only we'd had a young teacher like Monique, we'd be prattling away in French like natives.'

'That's as may be,' interrupted O.L. 'but we can't stay here all day listening to tales of your mis-spent youth. Now Bert has recovered, we need to make up for lost time.'

The path going down to *Charamillon* from here was muddy rather than rocky but frequent slithers by Joyce and Penny made progress only marginally quicker than before.

Bert fared little better but all three found the descent amusing rather than alarming. As more and more blue sky replaced cloud to reveal the sun, morale was high when they arrived without mishap above the cable-car station and with time to spare.

'I think we've earned a coffee,' called Bert. 'And it'll give Joyce a chance to scrape the mud off her legs. We can't take her back to the hotel looking like that.'

'Cheeky monkey,' retorted Joyce. 'I'm not the only one looking the worse for wear. What you need, Bert, is a hose down to shift the mud stains on the back of your shorts. If they've got a high pressure hose, I'll do it for you myself with pleasure.'

'If that doesn't work, we could always call at the garage and put him in the car wash,' suggested Penny helpfully.

'Before anyone scrubs up,' cried Harry, 'I want a group photo in the same place as before with everybody in the same positions. Bert front row middle like last time.'

'With his back to the camera, of course,' added Joyce. 'It would be an awful pity not to see those colourful stains on his posterior.'

At the chalet-restaurant, the waiter again agreed to take a group photo, providing it didn't take as long as before. As surface water began to evaporate in the sun's heat, a cloud of mist rising from the valley below threw into sharp relief the snowy peaks on the skyline. Harry thought a shot like that would make an excellent follow-up to the photos of the storm he'd taken at the refuge. By the time he'd taken several shots from different angles, the mist had thickened and was swirling round the terrace. Bert had put on his anorak and O.L. was urging the others to drink up and start heading for the cable car.

'Hold on Olive,' cried Harry, 'I haven't started my coffee yet and we're not all here, are we? Where are Joyce and Penny? Still inside sprucing themselves up, I expect.'

O.L marched off to round them up but returned a few minutes later to announce that she hadn't been able to find them.

'How can anyone get lost in a restaurant?' she exclaimed. 'It's not possible.'

When two figures loomed up from outside the terrace, she rushed forward to demand an explanation.

'Sorry, everybody,' called Penny. 'We took the wrong door coming out. We've been all round the chalet looking for you in this mist.'

'You had us worried there, Joyce,' said Harry. 'We thought you'd made a rendez-vous with that very obliging young waiter.'

'No such luck,' replied Joyce wistfully. 'We'll just have to make do with old codgers like you and Bert.'

The mist had lifted when they got down to *Le Tour* but the prospect of waiting thirty minutes for a bus didn't appeal to O.L. After consulting her map, she asked if anyone fancied walking down to *Argentière* on the *Petit Balcon Nord*. It was only about two kilometres and they could catch the bus or a train from there.

Harry's first instinct was to reject O.L.'s idea without hesitation but when Monique said it was a lovely walk and downhill all the way, he had a sudden change of mind.

'I'm up for it,' he cried. 'No point getting back early. A gentle stroll on a pleasant summer's evening, what could be nicer? It'll be the icing on the cake! The perfect end to an exhilarating day! All in favour?'

O.L. was not the only one to be taken aback by Harry's readiness to prolong the walk. Joyce and Penny had relied on him to put a brake on O.L. rather than back her up. Not so surprised were Mavis and Bert, both of whom saw the link between Monique's vote in favour and Harry's apparently spontaneous endorsement.

Joyce and Penny felt they had done enough for one day but when everyone else nodded in agreement, they reluctantly shouldered their rucksacks.

'After crossing the stream which drains the *glacier du Tour*, we reach the charming hamlet of *Le Planet*,' stated Monique. 'Then we shall see the moraine of the *glacier d'Argentière*.'

'Sounds great,' exclaimed O.L. 'More wonderful views. Let's get moving.'

O.L.'s euphoria was short-lived. The stream coming down from the glacier turned out to be a raging torrent which had burst its banks, leaving the footbridge stranded, surrounded by a wide area of swirling, muddy water.

'I hope you're not going to suggest we wade through that lot, Olive,' exclaimed Joyce. 'Count me out if you are: I've had enough of water today.'

O.L. hated to concede defeat but Monique was adamant. Attempting to cross the bridge in conditions like that would be foolish. They would have to go back. They still had time to catch the bus.

'At least it'll make a good photo, Olive,' cried Harry. 'Don't move. I want you in the foreground. Look at the bridge. Raise your arms in despair. Perfect. Could be a winner, that one. I'll call it 'Frustration.' Sums it up nicely, don't you think?'

O.L. agreed before striding off to join the others on their way back to *Le Tour*.

Sitting next to Harry in the bus, Mavis said that frankly she was not too bothered about having to turn back from the bridge. What's more, she didn't think Harry was either.

'Between you and me, Mavis, I wasn't. I only supported O.L. because of Monique. When she seemed keen to go further, I couldn't disappoint her, could I?'

'Disappoint, Harry? Don't you mean you wanted to impress her? Isn't that why you agreed to come with us to Chamonix? Show her how fit you were? In spite of being nearly twice her age.'

'You could be right there,' replied Harry thoughtfully. 'It was seeing her with those three young climbers that did it. I wanted to show I was just as fit and keen as they were. She's a lovely girl, Monique, but I can see now, I'm fighting a losing battle.'

'Not to worry, Harry, you'll get over it. I'll buy you a beer when we get to the hotel to drown your sorrows.'

Before leaving to drive home, Monique said she was going to see a film that evening about Nepal. It was being shown in *La Maison de la Montagne* in Chamonix and started at 9 o'clock. Would anyone like to join her? First to raise a hand was O.L., followed closely by Harry, Mavis, Betty, Mike and Joe. Monique said she could take the three ladies into town by car; as for the men, it would only take them about twenty minutes to get there on foot.

'What about you, Bert?' inquired Harry when Bert joined Mavis and himself in the bar. 'Having an early night, are you? Getting your strength up for the big one tomorrow? Nearly 1200 metres of climbing! Think you'll make it?'

'Never mind about me, Harry old son, I'll make it all right,' replied Bert. 'What about yourself? You're pushing the boat out, aren't you, going into Chamonix after dinner? You won't get to bed much before midnight. Not taking pep pills, are you? Or is the presence of the lovely Monique enough to keep your legs moving?'

'Now you come to mention it, Bert, I do find my legs considerably invigorated in the presence of the lady in question. Now what about that beer you owe me?'

'Talking about Monique,' said Mavis, 'I think we've got to buy her something. We've all appreciated the way she's looked after us and led the walks. Any suggestions?'

'It so happens,' replied Harry, 'I thought about that before we left home and I've brought her a copy of 'Fellwalking with Wainwright.' She'll enjoy reading a book in English about walking, especially one with such magnificent photos of the Lake District.'

'Brilliant, Harry,' exclaimed Mavis. 'I've heard her say she'd love to walk in the Lake District. She'll be delighted. I'll think of something else to add to it.'

As they left the bar to shower and change for dinner, Bert hoped Harry wouldn't have too much of a struggle getting to his room on the top floor. If he needed another stick …

Harry would have preferred to soak himself in a hot bath but a shower revived him and he resisted the temptation to stretch out on his bed for a nap. After forcing himself to do one of the exercise routines recommemded by his personal trainer, he felt a glow of self-satisfaction. He was fitter than he'd ever been. His performance had surprised everyone, not least himself. Gladys, back home, would be proud of him … and pleased to learn there'd been no major disputes between himself and O.L. Thinking of Gladys, Harry remembered his promise to keep in touch and decided to send an e-mail to her at once. After describing Joyce collapsing into the arms of Mike, the spectacular storm, the slippery descent and Bert's fall on the rocks, he suddenly had an idea. If Mrs Williams, the lady whose baby Bert had pulled out of the burning car, really wanted to reward him, she could offer to buy him a pair of new boots! Would Gladys tactfully suggest this to her?

Harry's arrival at the dinner table in another new shirt caused Bert to shield his eyes.

'That's even worse than the one you wore the other day!' he exclaimed. 'All those squares, triangles and circles in flashy colours! You look like you belong to a circus!'

'I must say I've always fancied being a ringmaster,' replied Harry pensively, 'bringing a bit of colour into this drab world. I think I've missed my vocation, don't you?'

'Well you don't look like an undertaker, that's for sure,' responded Bert.

'More like your court jester, I'd have thought,' contributed Syd.

'Can't imagine Harry doing cartwheels and somersaults,' said Joyce. 'but I can see him as a stand-up comic ... with Bert as his side-kick.'

Monique's cry *à table, les enfants,* put an end to the banter as they took their seats at the garden table in warm sunshine. Bert found the leek and potato soup much to his liking and didn't waste time talking. Asked by Joyce if he'd like a third helping, he accepted, saying 'yes, if nobody else wants to finish it off' ... but without waiting to see if anyone else did.

The arrival of the next course, *truite aux amandes*, complete with head and tail, raised a few eyebrows and sent a shudder through Penny. Allergic to fish, she had ordered an *omelette aux fines herbes* but the smell and the sight of the trout being topped, tailed and boned proved too much for her. Excusing herself, she moved to another table with her omelette and was happy to stay there, nursing the hotel's Siamese cat, until all traces of trout debris had been removed and dessert was being served.

'About our climb tomorrow to *La Jonction*,' said Monique, 'there is a lttle problem. I had thought we would take the chair-lift from *Les Bossons* and start our walk from *Le Chalet du Glacier* at 1410 metres.'

'Oh no,' exclaimed Joyce, 'not a chair-lift! I couldn't face going up in one of those contraptions. I don't think Penny could either.'

'I realise that, Joyce,' replied Monique. 'The problem is that if we avoid the chair lift and start lower down at the hamlet of *Le Mont*, we'd have 254 metres more to climb.'

'I don't see much of a problem there,' interrupted O.L. 'That would only take us 45 minutes.'

'45 minutes to get up and 30 to come down, don't forget,' pointed out Mavis. 'According to my calculations, that would make the walk take at least 7½ hours. And the total amount of ascent would be in excess of 1400 metres.'

'1400 metres of climbing!' gasped Penny. 'That's about twice what we've done today! I'll never make it.'

Monique said she had never thought they would all make it. *La Jonction* was one of the most beautiful walks in the valley but it wasn't for everyone. Even if they took the chair-lift, they would find it a long hard walk with steep and rocky sections.

'What I propose,' she went on, 'is to start from *Le Mont* – my uncle has offered us his minibus which I will drive – and walk up to the Chalet du Glacier. From here, a lovely path winds its way up through the trees to the Chalet des Pyramides. It's a climb of 485 metres that should take us less than two hours. We could have refreshment on the *terrasse panoramique* overlooking the *Glacier des Bossons* with its seracs and ice pyramids and then decide who would like to continue to *La Jonction.*'

'Sounds great,' cried Harry. 'No chair lift to worry Joyce and Penny and the option of a leisurely lunch and long siesta to suit Bert. Just as a matter of interest, Monique, how much further away is *La Junction?*'

When Monique said there was a further 690 metres of climbing which she thought would take about 2½ hours, Harry looked less enamoured, which didn't go unnoticed by O.L.

'That'll sort out the sheep from the goats,' she muttered sotto voce to Mavis.

'One more thing,' said Monique. 'I'd like to make an earlier start tomorrow. Can you all be ready to depart at 8.30? Now I think it's time to leave for Chamonix.'

As he was leaving with Mike and Joe, Harry wished Joyce and Penny a pleasant evening looking after Bert: he should be put to bed at 10 o' clock sharp when they could read him his favourite bedtime story, The Tale of Peter Rabbit.

Bert said he liked the ides of a bedtime story but would Joyce and Penny mind waiting until the football match on TV had ended at about 11?

When the answer was an emphatic no, Bert shrugged his shoulders and said it was a pity. He hoped Harry wouldn't nod off during the film show and, more importantly, would remember to remove his boots when he got back at midnight before crawling upstairs.

Bill and Syd had pricked up their ears at the mention of a televised football match but when they found out it was soccer not rugby, they decided they would sooner remain in the garrden and play chess by moonlight. With

Joyce and Penny opting for an early night, Bert joined three more football fans in the bar where Bill and Syd found him an hour later, alone and fast asleep.

LA JONCTION

'I hear you managed to get to sleep last night without a bedtime story, Bert,' said Harry during breakfast.

'No problem, Harry,' replied Bert briefly, without elaborating. 'Slept like a log. How about you? I hope you haven't signed up for a trek in Nepal next year. You'll have your work cut out today, as it is. Harry Birch climbing 1400 metres? I'd sooner bet on Accrington Stanley winning the FA cup!'

'Stranger things have happened, Bert old son,' retorted Harry. 'You could be in for a surprise. I expect at least a can of beer from you at *La Jonction* – assuming, of course, that you ever get there to give it to me.'

'Everybody got picnics, plenty of water, sun lotion and sunglasses?' called O.L 'And don't forget your sticks or poles.'

'We're not taking picnics, Joyce and I' answered Penny. 'There's no way we'd get up to *La Jonction* so we're going to have a leisurely lunch under a parasol at the chalet.'

'While you're sweating it out plodding onwards and upwards,' added Joyce.

O.L. sniffed disdainfully at this remark: the return trip to *La Jonction* from the *Chalet des Pyramides* could take four hours and she hoped Penny and Joyce wouldn't get bored waiting for their return.

'You don't need worry about that, Olive,' replied Joyce. 'After our leisurely lunch, we'll soak up the views, sunbathe, have a siesta and read our novels: then it will be tea time.'

Monique drove through Chamonix and took the narrow winding road up to *Le Mont*.

After yesterday's storm, the sun was shining in a cloudless blue sky and the air was crisp and fresh as they took the path up though trees and along the ski piste to the viewpoint overlooking the *Glacier des Bossons*.

'It's in retreat,' said Monique, 'like all the other glaciers. A few years ago, the tongue of the glacier collapsed and began to melt: now, just in front of us, all we see is rubble. You'll be much more impressed higher up when we reach the *Chalet des Pyramides*.'

Joyce and Penny were disappointed that Harry didn't support their suggestion of a coffee stop at the *Chalet du Glacier*. The old Harry would not have hesitated.

'I think we might afford a five minute water stop,' was all he said. 'If we go in for coffee, we'll be there for 20 minutes at least. And we haven't walked an hour yet. Is that O.K. with you, Monique?'

Monique said it was fine by her but she wanted to call and say hello to the couple who ran the chalet. They were old friends of hers and she'd be back in a few minutes. Seizing the opportunity to talk about the presentation she had in mind, Mavis gathered the group together.

'I'm sure we'd all like to give Monique a token of our appreciation,' she began. 'I mentioned it last night to

Harry and he's brought with him a copy of 'Fellwalking with Wainwright' to give her on our behalf. Maybe we could all sign it in the bar before she arrives this evening. Then last night, to add to the book, I bought a DVD of the film on Nepal which she really enjoyed. Anyone got any more suggestions?'

'How about your old boots, Bert?' cried Harry. 'You're never going to go home in them, surely! Monique would be tickled pink if you left one of them with her. You could plant something in it – preferably something sweet smelling – like thyme or rosemary. She could fix it on her bedroom wall, next to my sheep-soiled baseball cap.'

Bert looked wistfully at his boots. There was no denying they were shot at.

'I've an idea for the other boot,' exclaimed Joyce. 'Plant a forget-me-not in it and stand it on the ashes of your old anorak, the one we cremated in the garden on Saturday. It'll be like a tombstone.'

When Monique rejoined them, she wanted to know why they were laughing.

'Just a little joke about Bert's boots,' said Harry. 'Somebody suggested donating them to the *Musée Alpin* before we go home tomorrow – if they survive today.'

The pace slowed as the gradient steepened but they were glad of the shade as the path zig-zagged through the forest. Once above the tree-line and exposed to the sun, Penny and Joyce were straggling as the heat began to take its toll and Monique called for a pause. For once, O.L. did not object. She had so far restrained her instinct to surge ahead and kept behind Monique. Harry wondered if she was beginning to feel the strain.

'Maybe she's seen the light at last,' speculated Mavis, 'and learned to pace herself in the mountains. Remember that proverb about looking after your horse if you've got a long way to go? I think she's got the message.'

'Taking it easy today, Olive?' called out Harry. 'Didn't miss your beauty sleep, did you, after watching the film? Not been climbing in the Himalayas all night, have you?'

'No, I slept as soundly as ever, thank you Harry. As for the film, I thought it was breathtaking. What impressed me, apart from the wonderful scenery, was the way those porters managed to carry such enormous loads on their backs. Scrambling over rocks wearing flip-flops! And some of them were women!'

'And they were so cheerful!' exclaimed Mavis. 'I liked their huge grins.'

'I bet a pound to a pinch of snuff that Nepal's already on your wish list, Olive,' cried Harry. 'After watching that film, I'm even tempted to go there myself.'

Bert considered this so implausible that he burst out laughing. O.L. also thought Harry was fantasizing but the very fact that he'd even contemplated going to Nepal impressed her.

On resuming, Monique urged caution as the narrow path contoured across steep slopes before rising sharply to reach the *Chalet des Pyramides* at 1895 metres. Built against a rock face, overlooking the glacier with its weirdly shaped seracs and ice pyramids, the chalet could not have been better situated. From the panoramic terrace, set out with tables shaded by colourful parasols, there were vertiginous views of the valley far below backed by the

Aiguilles Rouges. Above, rose the glacier heading towards *Mont-Blanc* with the jagged outlines of the *Aiguilles de Chamonix* on one side and the rounded *Dôme du Goûter* on the other. Harry wasted no time getting out his camera.

Joyca and Penny couldn't conceal their delight. The chalet itself, with its window boxes of red geraniums, looked inviting and it would be a pleasure spending the afternoon there. For the others, it was decision time, to stay at the chalet or to press on to *La Jonction,* almost 700 metres higher up. In the event, they all voted to continue and Monique clapped her hands in approval.

'Do you realise we'll be following in the steps of Balmat and Paccard? This is the route they took to make the first ascent of *Mont-Blanc* in 1786. They rested in a cave near the junction of the two glaciers, *Bossons* and *Taconnaz.* You'll see it on your map, Olive: it's called *le Gîte à Balmat.*'

Consulting her watch, she announced that it was 11.40, too early for lunch. If they kept up a steady pace, they would reach *La Jonction* about 14.00 and picnic there. She would like to leave in five minutes as soon as they had had a snack, drunk plenty of water and refilled their water bottles.

'No time for a beer now, Harry, You'll have to wait till we get back down.'

'What about the can you're going to give me at the top?' cried Harry.

'Sorry, old pal, I'm travelling light,' Bert replied. 'Couldn't see the point of carrying the extra weight when you're never going to get there.'

This confident assertion by Bert was all Harry

needed to strengthen his determination to reach *La Jonction,* come what may. Resisting the impulse to question Bert's own ability to make it, he shrugged his shoulders, finished eating his banana, transferred his bag of nuts and raisins from rucksack to trouser pocket, waved goodbye to Joyce and Penny and strode off to join Monique and O.L.

Ahead, dozens of zigzags stacked closely one above the other, snaked their way upwards. Joe calculated that for every two metres of height gained, they walked ten. Not that he bemoaned the fact: on the contrary he was full of admiration for the way the path had been engineered to produce a constant gradient and to prevent erosion. Monique kept religiously to the path, spurning the temptation to cut corners. On one occasion, she caught Bert taking a short cut at a bend and wagged her finger at him. By sticking to the path, he would maintain a steady rhythm and save energy: what's more, he wouldn't add to the erosion already caused by impatient walkers who didn't realise the consequences of cutting corners.

Harry didn't find the climb particularly tiring but the innumerable sharp bends left and right had a soporific effect on him. Plodding along like an automaton behind Monique and O.L., he felt as if he were sleep-walking. When the path straightened out, the rock-strewn landscape brought him down to earth and he had to concentrate on where he was putting his feet to avoid stumbling.

After an hour's steady climbing, Monique paused when they met the path coming up from Taconnaz. They had kept fairly well together and she was pleased with their progress.

'Still with us, Bert?' called Harry. 'Thought you might have gone back to join Penny and Joyce over a bilberry tart and coffee.'

'I'm all right, Harry, but what about you? You had me worried coming up those zigzags: you looked like a zombie.'

'Slow and steady, Bert, that's the best advice I can give you. You just switch off and your legs carry on like clockwork. Works like a charm. Takes the pain away. You should try it. And if you need any more help, I've plenty of nuts and raisins left.'

As the path became steeper, Harry couldn't hide the fact that he was feeling the strain. Red in the face, sweating profusely and gasping for breath, he found himself being overtaken by everyone except Betty and Mavis, they themselves struggling to keep up. It was only his grim determination to prove Bert wrong that kept him on his feet.

After a short rock scramble, they contoured round below the *Mont du Corbeau* to reach the *Gîte à Balmat* where Monique, to Harry's relief, called a second pause.

'*Bon courage, tout le monde*,' she called gaily. 'Only another twenty minutes to go. We'll picnic overlooking the junction of the two glaciers.'

'I could eat a horse,' cried Bert, 'and Harry looks like he needs one. Are you O.K., Harry? You look drained. I think you've had enough. Why not wait here and we'll pick you up on the way down?'

'There's nothing wrong with me that a few minutes' rest won't cure,' replied Harry. 'Just thought I'd keep Mavis and Betty company for a while. Saving myself for the last lap.'

Bert found this explanation far from convincing but when Harry resumed his place behind Monique and O.L. and showed no sign of flagging for the next twenty minutes, he had to admit Harry had won the day.

On arriving at the signpost announcing *La Jonction, 2589 m*. Harry insisted on a group photo, overruling Bert who wanted to eat straight away, saying he was ravenous.

'We can't have a group photo without you on it, Harry,' cried Monique. 'I'll ask one of those people over there to take it with you.in the middle between Olive and myself.'

It was almost 2.30 before the photo had been taken to Harry's satisfaction and they sat down to picnic on one of the flat slabs of rock nearby. The setting was awesome: covering an area of about 4 square kilometres, the glacier was almost completely enclosed by high mountains, culminating in *Mont-Blanc* at 4807 metres Monique pointed out one of the classic routes to the summit via the *Refuge des Grands Mulets,* built on a rocky island halfway across the glacier. The other and more popular route was via the *Refuge du Goûter* and the *Dôme du Goûter* which they could see prominently ahead at 4304 metres. O.L. hung on Monique's every word. Names like these were music to her ears. After both she and Harry had located the places on her map, they left the others still eating, to go and take photos. Mavis thought she'd never seen Olive and Harry so pally: they seemed to be on the same wavelength at long last.

Harry was well pleased with his performance. He didn't know how he'd managed the last lap: his legs had felt like lead and his breath had been laboured. Mind over matter, he supposed. The determination to make Bert eat his words.

'Well Bert,' he said, 'Here I am, sound in wind and limb, at *La Jonction*. Never thought I'd get here, did you? Or was that just an excuse for not bringing me a beer?'

'Sorry about that, my old mate, didn't think you had it in you. Mind you, nobody else did either. You've amazed us all. I'll get you that beer when we get back to Joyce and Penny.'

'That will take us about 1½ hours,' said Monique, 'and then it will take another 1½ hours to get down to *Le Mont*. I'm glad we came by minibus and don't have to hurry down to catch the last chair-lift.'

'Think your knees can survive 1400 metres of descent, Harry?'

'I would say that my knees have a much better chance of survival than your boots, Bert,' replied Harry. 'It would be a shame if they fell apart before you had a chance to donate them to a worthy cause.'

'O.K. everyone?' called Monique. 'Don't hurry on the way down and no cutting corners, please, Bert.'

O.L. seemed quite content to keep behind Monique on the way down just as she had done on the way up. Not only that: she didn't paw the ground with impatience whenever they stopped to wait for stragglers. She had even raised a smile at the chit-chat between Harry and Bert which she usually found irritating. Nor had she shown any resentment at not being consulted about presents for Monique. On the contrary, she couldn't have approved more of Harry's choice of book, 'Fellwalking with Wainwright' was a favourite of hers.

'But Harry,' she said, 'I didn't know you were a fan of Mr Wainwright,'

'I wouldn't go so far as that, Olive,' replied Harry. 'Up to now, I've always found him a bit too energetic for my taste. Let's just say I've begun to warm to him lately. What a pity he never came to walk in the Alps and write guidebooks. They would have made fascinating reading.'

'I'm sure they would,' said Olive pensively. 'You know he did plan a walking tour in 1938 of the Bernese Oberland. He wrote a detailed programme to give to his friends but the outbreak of war made this impossible.'

Listening to this talk between them, it occurred to Mavis that both Harry and Olive had changed considerably in the past week. Olive had become more relaxed and less judgemental and Harry had become more ready to compromise. Gladys would be delighted to learn of their rapprochement – if it survived the journey home.

All went well until they reached the stacked up series of zigzags above the *Chalet des Pyramides*. Still behind Monique and O.L., Harry again felt like an automaton as he negotiated one sharp turn after another, time and time again but his trance-like state was shattered by a shout from Mike, higher up. Bert had apparently ground to a halt: the sole of his left boot, such as it was, had become detached from the toecap. Monique, O.L. and Harry went back up to find Bert sitting on a rock and Mike inspecting the damaged boot.

'I don't suppose anyone's got any superglue, have they?' cried Mike. 'No? Maybe they'll have some at the chalet. I think the best we can do now is tie the sole on with string.'

'Well Bert,' said Harry, 'I hope you don't need any more convincing that those boots have reached journey's end. When Mike's finished tying it on your foot, I'll take a photo for your bedside table and we'll give them the last rites tonight.'

As they approached the chalet, expecting to be greeted by cheers and applause, they were disappointed. Joyce and Penny were nowhere to be seen, either on the terrace or inside the chalet. It was the warden who put their minds at rest on two counts: Joyce and Penny had left to go down fifteen minutes ago and yes, he'd be able to stick the sole on Bert's boot.

'Good thinking, their going down ahead of us,' cried Harry. 'We can afford to give them a start. And there'll be time for that beer you owe me, Bert, while your boot's drying.'

Bert nodded, went over to the bar and returned to have a quiet word with Mavis.

'I've just bought a jar of honey. Thought of puttng it in this boot for Monique. What do you think?'

'Brilliant!' exclaimed Mavis. 'Leave the packing to me. She'll be delighted.'

Relaxing with their drinks under parasols on the terrace, no-one, least of all O.L., showed any inclination to catch up with Joyce and Penny, now ½ hour ahead of them.

Finally, to spur them on, Monique quoted from *La Fontaine's* fable about the hare and the tortoise, '*Rien ne sert de courir: il faut partir à point.*' Asked to explain, Mavis said it was no good running to catch up, the important thing was to start promptly. If they waited any longer, Joyce and Penny would arrive before them at the minibus.

As an added precaution, Mike had tied string round Bert's boot and there were no more delays on the descent through the forest to the *Chalet du Glacier*. Monique had half expected to find Joyce and Penny there but again there was no sign of them. When they didn't show up on the ski run after the chair-lift, Monique looked worried.

'They can't have got lost getting down to *Le Mont*, surely,' she cried. 'We should have caught them up by now.'

'Unless we've under-estimated them,' said Mike. 'After all, it was the tortoise that won the race. They're probably waiting for us at the minibus.'

To everyone's relief, Mike was right. Joyce and Penny were standing by the minibus chatting to two young men who had walked down with them from the *Chalet du Glacier*.

'What kept you?' cried Joyce. 'It's half past six! We were just thinking about calling Mountain Rescue.'

'You can blame Bert for the delay,' cried Harry, 'but we'll tell you all about that over dinner. Let's get back to the hotel or we'll not have time for a shower.'

On the way back, Monique said she would ask her uncle to defer dinner until eight o'clock: this would allow her more time to drive home, change and return to the hotel. She would also ring the taxi firm to confirm their departure for Geneva at nine a.m. next morning.

When she had left, Mavis suggested meeting in the bar at quarter to eight to sign the copy of 'Fellwalking with Wainwright' which Harry had brought for Monique.

In addition to that, there was the DVD of the film on Nepal which she had bought last night and Bert's boot, held together by superglue and string, in which he'd inserted a jar of alpine honey. Would Olive be kind enough to make the presentation after dinner?

'Nothing would give me greater pleasure,' exclaimed O.L. 'but the rest of us must be allowed to contribute if these gifts are on behalf of us all. How much shall we give you?'

'Speaking for myself,' replied Harry, 'Nothing. I think you feel the same, Mavis. As for your old boot, Bert, a jar of honey's well worth buying to get rid of it, wouldn't you say?'

'In that case,' said O.L. 'the remaining eight of us will have to buy something else.'

'What about some champagne,' suggested Bill, 'to celebrate the wonderful week we've had? If the eight of us contributed 10 euros each, we could buy two bottles to round off our last dinner tonight in style.'

O.L. looked dubious but when the idea was met by spontaneous enthusiasm from everyone else, she offered no objection. Bill passed his hat round to collect the contributions saying he would arrange everything with uncle Claude.

As they dispersed to go to their rooms, Bert took off his boots, giving one to Mavis together with the jar of honey and the other to Joyce who had envisaged it as a tombstone on the ashes of his cremated anorak.

Harry was in high spirits as he showered and changed. He had exceded his own and everyone else's expectations in reaching *La Jonction*. What also pleased him was a reply to his e-mail from Gladys. Mrs Williams would be delighted to buy new boots for Bert. She'd spoken to the manager of the outdoor shop and all Bert had to do was choose whatever boots he fancied.

When he appeared in the bar, scrubbed up, clean-shaven and sporting a new tartan shirt, Bert won an approving look from Joyce who consented to sit next to him when they went outside to the candle-lit table. O.L. was ushered to the head of the table by uncle Claude who inquired routinely if she had enjoyed her day as he poured out wine for her approval. Taking her nods and smiles as sufficient answers, he didn't wait for elaboration but scurried off to return with the first course, three huge dishes of *salade César*.

While Harry was reeling off the names of the ingredients – slivers of chicken, lettuce, hard boiled egg, anchovies, green beans, tomatoes, croutons and vinaigrette sauce – Bert made substantial inroads into the nearest dish and Joyce found it necessary to remind him that each dish contained four helpings. Apart from which, had he ever heard of the old expression 'ladies before gentlemen.' Bert apologised on the grounds that he'd eaten practically nothing all day and felt faint with hunger. Penny thought this highly unlikely but took pity on him and off-loaded her portion of chicken onto his readily outstretched plate.

She thought the salad was a meal in itself. When she wondered if she'd have room for the *tartiflette* to follow, Bert kindly offered to help her out if need be.

In the interval between courses, Joyce wanted to know why Harry blamed Bert for their late arrival at *Le Mont*. Had he fallen again as he'd done yesterday?

'No,' replied Harry, 'but it was a close run thing. One minute he's plodding serenely down the zigzags, no doubt thinking about the beer he's going to enjoy at the *Chalet des Pyramides*, next minute he's tottering about out of control like a drunk. Why, you ask? Because the wafer thin sole on his left boot had finally decided that enough was enough. Hanging on by a thread, it caused our dear friend Bert to stumble and lose his balance. Had his guardian angel not been hovering overhead, we might, at this very moment, ladies and gentlemen, be composing his epitaph.'

'Well, it hasn't affected his appetite, has it' commented Syd drily.

'Very true,' continued Harry. 'but it did slow us down. Picture the scene, ladies and gentlemen: Bert sitting on a rock on the edge of an abyss looking forlornly at his protruding toes. Relieved to see him still with us, we all gather round. Bert brushes off our concern: he is prepared to continue the descent bootless. Step forward the ever resourceful Mike. Delving into his rucksack, he produces a length of string and ties the sole back in place.'

'Only as a stop-gap measure,' interrupted Mike. 'I doubt if string would have held the boot together all the way down to the minibus. We were lucky they were able to stick the sole back on at the chalet.'

'So now poor old Bert's got to fork out for a new pair,' cried Joyce. 'You've salvaged the laces, I hope, Bert? Have another glass of wine to drown your sorrows.'

When the *tartiflette* appeared in individual earthenware dishes, Monique said it was another regional speciality consisting of strips of bacon, sliced potatoes and chopped onions covered with grated cheese which melted and turned brown in the oven.

'Looks and smells delicious,' exclaimed Bert. 'Don't ask for one without bacon, Penny, I'll take care of that.'

Hovering in the background, Claude was gratified to see how much they were finding the meal to their liking. No sooner had they all finished mopping up the last remaining traces of cheese than two more large dishes of *tartiflette* and two more bottles of wine arrived on the table. Harry took it upon himself to go round topping up glasses while Bert, ladle in hand, offered everyone carefully measured extra helpings, making up for his earlier lapse by serving himself last.

From her seat at the top of the table. O.L. surveyed the scene with satisfaction. Thurston Ramblers on their first ever trip abroad had acquitted themselves well. She looked forward to telling them so when the opportunity arose.

'Got any room left for apple tart and cream, Penny?' called Bert as the next dish appeared. 'You've hardly stuck to your diet this week, have you?'

'If you're angling for any more of my meal, you're wasting your time,' retorted Penny. 'And if you really want to know, I've put my diet on hold until tomorrow.'

'It's called *tarte tatin*,' explained Monique. '*C'est une tarte renversée*. In English, please, Mavis?'

When Mavis said it was an upside-down tart, Monique went on to say that the recipe had been discovered by chance. According to legend, one of the Tatin sisters who ran a hotel, overcooked the caramelized apples by mistake and decided to put the pastry on top of them. She then put the pan in the oven and when the pastry had turned brown, she turned the pan upside down onto a plate so that the apples came out on top.

'If it tastes as good as it looks, it'll be delicious,' cried Joyce. 'Take a photo of it, Harry before Bert gets a chance to spoil the picture.'

Harry needed no second invitation. He already had his camera at hand to capture the moment when Claude would appear with the champagne. Monique, who knew nothing about this arrangement, burst into applause on her uncle's arrival. Taking his cue from her, Harry did likewise whereupon the others followed suit, clapping and cheering as the corks popped and the bottles were opened.

While the glasses were being filled and passed round, Mavis slipped away to return with the presents for Monique which she put on the table in front of Olive.

Rising to her feet, O.L. began by saying she wouldn't detain them long. She just wanted to say what a splendid week they had enjoyed and to thank Monique on behalf of them all for making it possible. Walking in the Chamonix Valley had been a revelation to her personally and, she was sure, to everyone else in the group. The views of snow-capped mountains and vast glaciers had been breathtaking. Everyone had walked well in unfamiliar terrain and she was proud of them. Would they all raise their glasses to say *merci Monique* after which she would like to present to her some tokens of their appreciation.

When the cries of *merci Monique* had subsided and the toast drunk, Monique stepped forward to accept her presents. She was clearly delighted with the DVD of Nepal and thrilled with the book on the Lake District but she exploded into laughter when she found Bert's boot.

'It is very kind of you to offer me these wonderful gifts,' she managed to say. 'I am very touched. Thank you all very much. I am so pleased you have enjoyed coming to Chamonix. It has been a pleasure for me too. I have very much enjoyed your company.'

Harry waited for the applause to die down before getting to his feet.

'Mesdames, mesdemoiselles, messieurs,' he intoned pompously, knowing he could rely on the groan which followed. 'Not excluding Bert, of course. May I crave your indulgence just a moment more to second the words of our worthy president. I confess, as you are all aware, to having had misgivings about joining you here in Chamonix when the invitation from our friend Monique was first received.'

'Misgivings?' shouted Bert. 'You said you'd sooner stroll along the beach on Anglesey than climb mountains!'

'That, my dear Bert, was in an earlier incarnation. Since then, thanks to the persuasive powers of Mavis and, in no small measure, to the insistence of Monique, I have undergone, as you are all well aware, a renaissance. This renaissance, you will recall, at first manifested itself on the snow-covered slopes of Pen-y-ghent. Further confirmation was provided on Helvellyn, Skiddaw and Scafell Pike. The final proof of my re-birth, ladies and gentlemen, took place this very day, the ascent of *La Jonction*, a climb of some 1400 metres!'

Here, Harry paused to finish his champagne before resuming.

'Needless to say, I heartily endorse Olive's appreciation of our charming guide. Monique's organisatiom of our walks has been impeccable, her local knowledge invaluable and her patience exemplary. May I also express our thanks to Claude for his warm hospitality and excellent meals.'

In response to the unanimous cries of 'hear, hear,' Claude bowed graciously.

'Just one more thing, ladies and gentlemen,' continued Harry. 'You will all be pleased to learn that Bert has been offered new boots by Mrs Williams, the lady he pulled out of the burning car. This will come as a relicf to us all, will it not! As for his old boots, I'm sure he'll feel consoled by leaving one as a souvenir to Monique and the other as a tombstone on the ashes of his equally long-suffering anorak.'

There was more applause when Claude returned from the bar with a bottle of cognac, and a dozen profiteroles. Joyce and Penny, already a little unsteady, readily accepted both, following the lead of the men. O.L. her speech rather blurred, told Mavis and Betty it would be impolite to refuse and joined Monique in taking a glass.

During a lull in the conversation, Bill announced that last night, while waiting for Syd to make his moves at chess, he had ben visited by the muse. As a result, he'd composed a poem which he'd called, Ode to Harry. Would they like him to read it? Yes, they certainly would, came the reply although Bert had a reservation.

'Is it fit for mixed company,?' he wanted to know.'It won't make Joyce blush, will it?'

'It would no doubt make Shelley or Keats blush,' replied Bill, 'but not, I think, Joyce. Here we go then.'

Ode to Harry

Of all the ramblers in the club
Harry's the one you'll find in the pub,
Knocking back Guinness and chatting up birds,
A sociable fella and ne'er short of words.

In latest gear, he cuts a dash -
You cannot fault him for panache -
His shiny boots and flashy shirts
Are much admired, unlike Bert's

Alas, too fond of cakes and ale,
Harry begins to drag and trail.
If weather isn't warm and sunny
He'll not come out for love nor money.

And when he does, for good or ill,
He struggles up the slightest hill.
In vain does Olive turn about
To urge him pull his finger out.

And then one day – you'll not believe me -
He says he's up for Chamonix!
I kid you not! You may well jeer,
Harry Birch, a mountaineer??

Now what, you ask, caused this to pass?
I'll tell you, friends, it was a lass!
A lass whose Gallic charm and glamour
Left Harry in a huge dilemma.

But not for long: he smartens up, gets fit,
Takes classes to improve his French a bit,
Impresses all, stern Olive too.
Fairwell old Harry, hail Harry new!

He loses weight, cuts down on ale,
Strides briskly over hill and dale.
Climbs Pen-y-Ghent and Scafell Pike,
Come rain or snow, keeps pace with Mike.

The moral of this tale, says Syd,
If you would change as Harry did,
Is plain as bread and jam,
First find the lady; cherche la femme!

Even allowing for the uninhibiting effect of wine, champagne and cognac, Bill was gratified by the response of his audience. Joyce and Penny giggled uncontrollably, clinging on to each other for support. Bert beamed and no-one laughed louder than O.L. Harry himself found Bill's ode as amusing as anyone else.

'Just about sums you up, Harry, don't you think?' laughed Mavis. 'I'd like a copy for my scrapbook, Bill, when you've got time.'

'Seeing you're in such good voice, Bill,' called Harry, 'how about giving us a song? Better still, a duet from you and Syd. A Welsh folksong, like 'Sosban Fach,' for example. I've no idea what it's about but it's got a very catchy tune.'

Bill said the song was about the troubles of a harassed housewife and invited everyone to join in when they came to

'Sosban fach yn berwi ar y tân,
Sosban fawr yn berwi y llawr,
A'r gath wedi sgrapo Joni bach.'

When Bill and Syd burst into song and the rest of the group joined in on cue, diners elsewhere in the garden clapped and shouted *bis, bis*. Mike and Joe took this as an invitation, and launched into 'Bluebells of Scotland' and Harry, not to be outdone, conducted them all in a spirited rendering of 'Clementine.' Seeing that some of the diners were joining in the chorus, Harry invited them to sing something in French. They responded with *Chevaliers de la Table Ronde*, much to the delight of Bert who bellowed out *oui, oui, oui* and *non. non. non* louder than anyone else, each time *Goûtons voir* came round.

O.L. had the impression that the singing could go on all night. There was packing to be done and they had to be ready to leave promptly at 9 a.m. What about Auld Lang Syne, she suggested to Harry, as an appropriate way to end the evening. Harry agreed and led the singing with the other diners joining in with the French version, *Ce n'est qu'un au revoir.*

On the way back into the hotel, Mavis told Harry how much she'd enjoyed the evening and in particular how pleased she was to see O.L. and himself on such good terms.

'You're not the only one to have changed, you know,' she added. 'Olive's been much more relaxed today and this evening than I've ever seen her.'

'I've noticed,' replied Harry. 'Chamonix has been good for her.'

'It's been good for you too!' exclaimed Mavis. 'I

just hope relations between you both don't deteriorate when we get back home.'

'That, Mavis, is in the lap of the gods,' said Harry. 'We'll just have to wait and see.'